Cycle Racing:
Training to win

Cycle Racing: Training to win

Revised Edition

Les Woodland

PELHAM BOOKS · LONDON

PELHAM BOOKS

Published by the Penguin Group
27 Wrights Lane, London W8 5TZ, England
Viking Penguin Inc., 40 West 23rd Street, New York, New York 10010, USA
Penguin Books Australia Ltd, Ringwood, Victoria, Australia
Penguin Books Canada Ltd, 2801 John Street, Markham, Ontario, Canada L3R 1B4
Penguin Books (NZ) Ltd, 182-190 Wairau Road, Auckland 10, New Zealand

Penguin Books Ltd, Registered Offices: Harmondsworth, Middlesex, England

First edition published 1975
Revised edition published 1986
Paperback edition published 1988

Copyright © Les Woodland 1975, 1986 and 1988

Made and printed in Great Britain by Butler & Tanner,
Frome, Somerset

Typeset by Wilmaset, Birkenhead, Wirral.

A CIP catalogue record for this book is available from the
British Library.

To Stephanie — for helping me with life and other punctures

PICTURE CREDITS
The photographs in this book were taken by Graham Watson.
The line illustrations were drawn by Vanessa Julian Ottie.

Contents

1 A curse on all scientists

Remember those great days before science? All you were expected to do was go about life the way it suited you best and hope for success. So far as cycling was concerned, you just piled up miles until aches and stiffness were replaced by fitness. Then you raced on Sundays, usually a morning time trial sandwiched between two breakfasts. Wonderful life.

It's all different now, of course. Athletes on wheels they call cyclists nowadays. If you're not racing, you're training. And if you're not training properly, well, you might just as well take up pigeon keeping instead. What a rotten life.

The solution's in your hands, of course. Once you accept that science is here and there's precious little either of us can do about it, you're halfway there. By the time you realise that, you're most of the way to accepting it and using it to turn you from what you are into something very much better.

Now, this isn't a correspondence course in winning bike races. You won't sprout muscles by turning the pages and looking at the diagrams. But it can make you a better rider; it *will* make you a better rider, if you do what it says.

Between now and the index, we shall go a long way. We shall go further into what makes you tick than you've probably been before. You'll find new words and new ideas, some of them quite complicated. But it's worth while persevering because until you understand *why* you're doing something, it's difficult or impossible to do it well, or properly, or convincingly. Nothing is more dispiriting or pointless than a vague and targetless training schedule that promises everything and delivers nothing. Believe me, I know.

How times change . . . once, the idea of an American in the Tour de France would have been laughable. Now Jonathan Boyer (above) has ridden and finished and Greg LeMond has gone still better.

I am a failed racer who tried more crackpot schedules than anybody and lived to count the cost. I knew intimately the training habits of any top name you care to mention from the mid-sixties and I tried them all for no better reason than that they seemed to be doing okay on them.

But there was more to it than that. I was a great one for fads as well. When I heard that Jacques Anquetil rode with curved handlebars – ones that had no straight on either side of the stem – I too bought curved handlebars. I read somewhere that Raymond Poulidor, who followed Anquetil about in the manner of the crocodile pursuing Captain Hook, drank cold tea during races. I too drank cold tea during races. I disliked it intensely. But I drank so much that I lurched uncertainly round corners with the weight of all that beverage slopping about inside me like a storm at sea. Oh, the things I tried in my pursuit of the secret of success.

There were several reasons it all came to nothing. For one, I didn't train hard enough. Second, I wasn't determined enough. Third, I wasn't hard enough. And fourth, there is a nagging possibility that I was less than an athletically perfect specimen. Those are my excuses. Take note while you have the chance.

But don't be carried away with the idea that all we enthusiasts have the ability to be the next champion of the world. There wasn't a Bernard Hinault or Greg LeMond or Francesco Moser inside me, fighting to get out. You have to accept that they might not be inside you, either. We all have physiological limits. But the reassuring thing is that few of us ever get remotely near them. There is always a very good chance that you could be considerably better.

You could improve by going out each night with the local chain gang. You could get fitter by piling up mile after mile, like the old boys did. Like some people still do. The trouble is that it doesn't work quickly enough and it's not often a comfortable experience.

I remember something Bill James said. He raced in the 1930s and later on became a coach:

> I wince when I think of some of the get-fit ideas I followed as a teenager. One such bash stands out in my mind – the annual Corfe Castle run. There and back in the same day, 230 miles and all on fixed, of course.
>
> The last 30 miles or so were virtually done in an insensitive daze, but since the big boys – Fleming, Walters, Burgess, Pond, Hill – did this, you didn't question why.

Voila! In one short and graphic description, all the reasons against unthinkingly accepting other riders' unexplained and unreasoned training ideas. My one consolation is that I'm not the only crackpot who followed what the champions did and suffered as a result.

Well, enough of all this. These Confessions of a No-hoper aren't the reasons why you've got this book. Read on.

2 The overload effect

First of all, answer me a question. What is fitness? Everyone talks about it, but it's pretty hard to define it. A lot of top people have tried.

Roger Bannister, the first chap to break four minutes for running a mile, said it's a state of mental and physical harmony that lets someone carry on his occupation to the best of his ability with the greatest happiness. Well, that's fair enough. But Norman Sheil probably expressed it better. He used to be Britain's national coach, then he became Canada's national coach, and after that I lost track of him. But he reckoned that fitness was the ability to do something – anything – at a required level.

That means that fitness isn't just something to do with sport. You can be fit to stand at a factory bench, or to be a local radio disc jockey, or to get paid for running Club 18–30 holidays in Benidorm. Of course, in the terms that you and I know them, you do have to be rather fitter to ride a stage of the Tour de France than to take bookings for a Golden Oldies disco. But you get the point – everyone is fit for the activity he has to perform.

Disc jockeys aren't physically competitive, so they're all at much the same (usually low) athletic level. They're fit enough not to collapse over the turntables halfway through a booking and that's all that anyone asks. But the job of a racing cyclist is to win races and since only one person can win a race at a time, it'll go to the fittest on the day. To be certain it's you, you have to make sure your fitness gets greater and greater until you have more of it than anyone else skulking about on the start list.

Luckily, your body has a knack for doing this. Provided you pump in enough effort at one end, it'll respond at the other. And by way of a bonus, it'll give you a teeny bit more than you asked for.

Let me give you an example. If you break your arm, the place where the bone heals will eventually be the thickest of the whole length of bone and therefore the strongest. It's as if something inside you has concluded that you might very well go about trying to break your arm again and has reacted by making it more difficult. It accepts everything you do as the norm it's got to expect and it reacts by making it easier to do it again next time.

It's called the Overload Effect. No overload – no taking yourself just past your usual limits – means no increase in fitness. For instance, if you train by riding 22 miles in an hour over much the same route, your fitness will get to just that level and stay there. Not until you go faster will your fitness increase.

That's a chicken and egg problem. Without getting fitter, how do you ride faster to get fitter? This Great Mystery of Life – and others – will be explained in due time.

The point to remember is that you get the overload effect, and therefore greater fitness, only by making your training progressive. No progression equals no overload; no overload equals no increase in fitness; and that means no improved results.

Ask yourself now: when you pull on your training gear and set out on your bike, are you sure that the stint ahead will make you faster? Do you know what the training is supposed to be doing, to which parts of your body, and why and how? And when you get back afterwards, all sweaty and feeling vaguely sick, how sure are you that (despite the way you feel) you're fitter than you were when you set out – that it hasn't all been a waste of time?

A lot of riders only train at the same level that they race. Some even train well below it. They spend a lot of time training with riders who aren't as good as they are, bashing along in a chain gang. There may be *some* improvement, of course. But not really enough to justify all that effort, all that time, all that riding home alone in the dark when you're the first one to get a puncture.

If the other riders are slower than you, then the group is too weak to be of much benefit to you. If they're faster, you'll spend too much time hanging on to a back wheel. By the time you've finished, the average speed works out at 23 mph – pretty useless for anyone planning to race at 25 mph or even considerably more. There *are* advantages, but they're probably not what you'd expect.

You get, by and large, what you train for. In the popular jargon, training is specific to the activity. That is why cyclists do most of their training on a bike, runners run, and cricketers practise batting and bowling. There are times to break that rule to your own advantage but, generally, training on a bike won't make you a good footballer, and getting three trebles in a row at darts will do nothing for your ballroom dancing.

This, if it's any reassurance, is why cyclists do embarrassingly badly in Superstars competitions. There can't be many sports more specific than balancing on wheels and stamping on pedals. And few athletes (in the widest sense of the word) either race or train as much as cyclists. So bike riders are good at whizzing up and down bankings, or round factory estates, but waddle round like Boer War veterans in running races.

Runners and footballers do better in general competitions because they spend much more of their training time on two feet, in varied activity. Car racers, who compete even less, have to do all their physical jerks out of the car cockpit and therefore have very unspecific training, and are simply ace Superstars. Which all goes to show just how specific your fitness is.

On the other hand, your body doesn't think for itself. Go running, or circuit training, or weight training, and it'll catch on pretty quickly. And provided you ride around a bit in the same few days that you do all these other activities, some of the more general benefits will transfer. And that, simply, is the concept of Transfer of Fitness.

Not everything switches over, of course. Do a lot of circuit training and next to no bike riding and you'll become just a rather talented circuit trainer. But mix the two and the benefits will show on your bike as well.

Your body is so good at this that it has another little trick in its repertoire. Should you ever have a leg in plaster after breaking it, the hospital will give you exercises for the unbroken leg. Break the left leg, exercise the right. Don't ask me why, but exercise to the healthy leg will have some benefit to the other one as well. From which you may safely conclude that your body is a very clever thing indeed.

You get fitter as the progression continues, provided the progression's not too fast. You can't go from one end of the training scale to the other in the space of a five-day week. Try that and you'll be flat on your back. But while the progression continues steadily, so fitness will rise on a constantly shallowing climb. But it has to be repeated exercise.

One night a week just brings you false confidence and aching legs. Three times a week is reckoned to be the minimum, including the race (which is just more training so far as your body is concerned). At that rate, you bring up the fitness curve fairly slowly. The more and the harder you train, the faster you climb the curve, but conversely the more time you need to rest. So there is only so much training you can do in a week.

Stop training, and fitness falls off at about the rate you acquired it, depending on where you are on the fitness curve.

At the very basic level – double-glazing salesmen, Punch and Judy men, etc – fitness is nothing more than basic good health. No coughs, no sneezes and no terminal cramps after running for a bus and they can lean against the bar, tap their stomachs and say 'Oh yes, keep myself pretty fit, y'know.' It means just having clear eyes and being able to change a wheel on the Mk3 Cortina without getting out of breath.

But surely there's more to it than that? Science is supposed to be *complicated*, for heaven's sake. All right, let's make it complicated.

Fitness is a combination of quite separate but often interlocked parts, most (or all, depending on how much attention you paid at school) spelled with an 'S': skill, stamina, speed, strength and psychology.

Skill

Jobs-we-would-all-like department . . . There was once a bunch of university boffins who had this idea that the more you did something, the better you might get at it. This might seem obvious, but what else are our universities for?

They, and other boffins elsewhere who'd chanced on this astonishing theory over the years, busied themselves and their students with all manner of repeated trials involving dismantled alarm clocks and the pushing of wheelbarrows along planks. And, to their surprise if not ours, they found they were right: the more you practised, the more you got the hang of it.

I don't know what they called it, but I'd call it skill. You need it to ride a bike, stay upright on roller skates, or teach a budgie to talk. After a lot of practice and occasional unfortunate surprises, you get better at it. You don't claim to be the best, but you're an expert. You're skilled.

Your first skill is balance. You can't ride a bike without it. From there you learn to pedal properly and gradually the thousands, millions, of pedal strokes get smoother and smoother until in the end you do it without thinking about it. You don't need to flip up a filing card in your brain for your nervous system to find out what it has to do. It's automatic. The brain sends signals down the nerves, the nerves tweak off the muscles, the muscles turn the pedals, and you go on for hours on end.

Pretty soon, you can ride the same distance with less cost in energy.

In the dark ages, when training was just a matter of going out and battering yourself senseless over hundreds and hundreds of miles ('It's only starting to do you good once you've done 80 miles' etc), there were really only a few things happening. There was the surplus fat being burned off. And there was the skill of pedalling economically, relearning skills lost in the winter lay-off.

Anything much else that happened was due to local muscular endurance (which we'll be getting to) and things like improvements in the weather. Some time triallists still work that way. After training at only relatively slow speed over long distances, their skill improves, their muscular endurance increases, and they acquire another skill as the season goes on: they learn to pace themselves over the distance. You can gain a lot in a time trial by riding so that your last ounce of energy burns up right on the line instead of five miles from home, leaving you a trembling heap at the roadside.

You probably remember how your second '25' time was much faster than your first, even though you did no appreciable training in between. It was because you got to grips with the distance; you knew what to expect.

Road racing needs skill, too. The ability to ride close up in a bunch, for example. The control to sprint in a straight line and thereby not bring down the whole bunch in the first race of the season.

Some sports haven't really got much further than training for skill. Cricket's a good example. I don't decry it; I simply remind you that cricketers are exceptionally skilful and still talk of cricket practice rather than cricket training, which has an odd sound about it. There is very little strength involved and only the bowler shows speed or endurance, which still come second to skill.

Perhaps a bowler could bowl faster, or a batsman strike out harder, if they combined their skill training with weight training to improve their strength. But they don't and nor, for that matter, do some cyclists.

An activity that requires solely skill comes closer to being a pastime or hobby than a sport. Ballroom dancing, synchronised swimming, darts and snooker are all exceptionally skilful but by that definition they cannot be classified as sports.

Skill is obviously the most specific of the S's, and the more skill you need for your chosen speciality, the less likely you are to be able to apply it to anything else. Certificates for medieval lute playing count for nothing when it comes to winning the *News of the World* darts championship.

Stamina

Posh people call this 'endurance', and that's the word you'll find in all the scientific textbooks. But endurance doesn't start with an S and it would mess up my idea for this book. So for now it's stamina.

There's no point in entering an 80-mile race if you can't complete the distance at any speed, let alone the speed of the winner. You have to know that your body can work long enough and hard enough.

Now, think about how your body works. You breathe in air, the blood collects the oxygen from the lungs and takes it, mixed up with sugars from the digestive system, to the muscles. It's an explosive mixture and an electrical signal from the brain, carried along the nerves, fires it off. Each explosion shortens a bundle of fibres inside the muscles and the greater the number and range of contracting muscle-fibre bundles, the more the muscles move.

The oxygen and sugar turn into carbon dioxide and waste and are carried back around the body in the veins.

If you don't ask too much of yourself, this natty arrangement will go on quite happily without your having to worry about it. But once you start getting all sorts of sporty ambitions, the system comes under strain.

First of all, the blood can't pick up all the oxygen the muscles need. The tiny air sacs – the alveoli – in the lungs are either blocked or unused to doing the job they were designed for. And when the blood, oxygen and sugar get to the muscles, they burn up more quickly than the veins can get rid of the rubbish.

When the lungs can't work quickly enough, you get out of breath and your throat tightens up. When the rubbish can't get out of the muscles, everything turns acidic and the muscles ache.

The speed at which your blood can suck oxygen through the thin membrane that separates it from your lungs is called oxygen uptake. It's obviously important to all endurance sports, like cycling, and it's used for that reason as a common measure of what's called core fitness.

The overload effect means that oxygen uptake improves as you increase the demands on your lungs. Cycling ranks high in the core fitness league, along with rowing, swimming and decathlon.

Men can make more use than women of their oxygen supply because their blood contains more haemoglobin – the part of the blood which carries the oxygen to the muscles. A man's blood contains between 4.6 and 6.2 million red corpuscles (which carry the haemoglobin) but a woman's holds only 4.2 to 5.4 million. This is one of several reasons why women are outpaced by men in sport.

The practical efficiency of your lungs is unlimited. They're much bigger than you'll ever need, for one thing, and if you stretched them out flat they'd more than cover a tennis court. They contain around 750 million alveoli (air sacs) and the more active you are, the more alveoli you can bring into use. Many of them you will never use. Others will become clogged through smoking or from dust or other impurities, and it's that muck that gets you coughing if you start any stressful activity suddenly after a lay-off.

The oxygen gets through the membrane and into the blood by a magical system called osmosis, which is all to do with differing pressures on either side of a permeable screen. The more you expand your rib cage and flex your diaphragm, the more air you drag in; the more alveoli you can use, the more oxygen you'll get into the blood and, of course, the more carbon dioxide you can breathe out.

The other equation of stamina happens in the muscles themselves. It's there that the complicated scientific process which turns oxygen and sugar into movement occurs.

Put simply, if more basic material can get into the muscles than can get out, the process gets blocked and the muscles become starved of oxygen. An acidic process then sets up and everything starts hurting. The ache is a protest and a warning.

The more you pedal, the more efficiently the blood will flow through the capillaries and the longer you will be able to continue without the pain becoming too bad. That's known as local muscular endurance, for the very good reason that it's local to the particular limb, it's muscular, and it's all about the endurance – the stamina or long life – of the activity.

This would all be very simple if your body used only one system of producing energy – the one I have described. Unfortunately, it doesn't.

If you think about it, it's obvious that there has to be a back-up system. If straightforward oxygen uptake controlled what you were doing, you'd have to start breathing more deeply *before* you were capable of increasing the activity. You'd first take a deep breath, then start running. After all, your rib cage pumps stale blood out of the veins and into the heart. From there it goes through the lungs to pick up more oxygen, back into the other side of the heart, and from there out through the arteries to the muscles.

But you can run without taking a deep breath first. You can run and at the same time hold your breath. In fact, many world-class sprinters – both cycling and running – don't breathe at all in the few seconds that they're racing. So something else must be happening.

Absence of oxygen doesn't stop a muscle working, but it does produce an oxygen debt. It's very complicated, but a circular system of alternative muscle energy means muscles can work for about 15 seconds entirely without oxygen but using chemicals known as ATP and ADP. These come from glucose stored in the muscles and they eventually produce lactic acid.

This system can operate hand-in-hand with straightforward oxygen work. Working with oxygen is called aerobic activity; working

Long climbs take you to the limit of oxygen uptake. The speed's fairly low so a streamlined position is less important than an uncramped one to let your diaphragm work. Marc Madiot leads Sean Kelly, in the Tour de France

without it is anaerobic. Once you get to about three-quarters of your maximum output, part of the energy will be produced anaerobically. At full effort – as in sprinting – the system will be entirely anaerobic.

The penalty of anaerobic activity is the lactic acid that pours into the blood, and since muscles work on protein, and protein can't function (or at least the muscle cells can't function) above a certain degree of acidity, lactic acid is bad news. Too much lactic acid and the muscle cells just stop working in protest and everybody rides away from you.

Even after you ease up, lactic acid still keeps flooding out. And that means it takes proportionately longer to recover from any exercise that's within a quarter of your maximum ability.

As a matter of interest, the worst thing you can do to recover when your body's throbbing with lactic acid and you feel dreadful is to stop altogether. 'Warming down' – continuing to ride slowly – is important because lactic acid disperses better at low rates of body activity than with the body at a complete standstill.

The more you train at below the anaerobic level – at close to but not over 75 per cent of your total ability – the more the overload effect will force back the oxygen debt barrier.

Fig. 1 Demands for stamina training

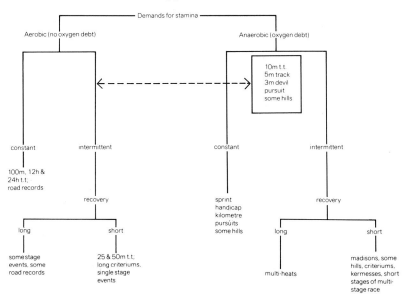

Stamina, therefore, is the efficiency with which you use and get rid of fuel, and being able to put out great and consistent effort without running into excessive oxygen debt.

How much stamina you need depends on the races you ride. A schoolboy belting round a park for five miles obviously has different requirements from a grizzly old veteran riding a '24'. And although cycling at almost any distance is an endurance sport, many coaches would argue that too many riders are doing too much endurance or stamina training. Which takes us back to getting in the miles as a way of training.

Once you can ride the race distance at any appreciable speed, your quest for stamina will inevitably take you to the next stage . . .

Speed

The trouble with speed is that it's relative. Cars in the Indianapolis Grand Prix lap at about 190 mph. And if he could hold the pace for long enough, the holder of the world speed record for a motor-paced bicycle would do quite well at, say, Silverstone. Because there the fastest laps are at 140 mph, compared to the 138.6 mph of the man on a bicycle.

Yet any of those figures seems slow when you look at a Porsche racing car – the 917/30 Can-Am – which can get from a standstill to 200 mph in less than 13 seconds and has a recorded top speed of 257 mph.

Look at cycling: the gold medal for riding 4,000 m in 1964 went at 29.36 mph. In 1980 – not that long afterwards in human terms – it was up to 32.55 mph. The contrasts continue: top-class track sprinters may nudge 40 mph in their last 200 m, but the record for the 24 hours is only just more than half that. And yet would a track sprinter have difficulty riding more than 500 miles in 24 hours? You see what I mean?

And yet we all know what speed is. It's the quality the winner has most of, and of which the runners-up need more.

The odd thing is that the difference in speed between the winner and the second, even the twentieth, rider is just about next to nothing. It's not as if several miles an hour separate them. Even in the Tour de France, the longest sporting event on earth, the difference between the first two men is well into decimals of one mile.

It's very galling to finish second or further back in a long race and realise this. You get a distinct feeling of 'if only . . .' At some point in the race, the winner went almost imperceptibly faster than you did, and that was that.

In a time trial, winning means just a fractionally higher cruising rate sustained all through the race. But in a road race, it can be just a tiny burst of energy that sees the break get clear – because a breakaway group, once clear, needs go no faster than the chasers to keep its advantage.

When you talk about speed in training, though, it's important to realise just what speed is. I heard that question asked at a national coaching course once and the answers were quite revealing. A lot of people said they could hold their top speed for 10 miles, citing their best '10' times and comparing them to a '25' or even the average of a road race. And yet, as you've seen, it's almost impossible to ride much more than 500 metres or so at more than 75 per cent maximum effort. At that degree of effort, you remember, the muscles start producing lactic acid and this, in the end, stops you carrying on at that speed.

High-speed cruising demands total concentration, the use of every available muscle, and superb oxygen uptake. Phil Anderson goes it alone.

If speed is what you get from a 100 per cent effort, it has to be the highest speed you can reach *before* lactic acid and oxygen debt make it impossible to continue, and that means the speed you'd get to in a 200-metre sprint. Short of tucking in behind a lorry, you just won't get any faster on the flat. And unless you're prepared to ride to your utmost for such short distances, over and over again, you'll never be as fast as you could be.

In Holland, where nearly all races are round short circuits through housing estates and villages, your average criterium is little more than repeated cornering and sprinting. And as a result, when it comes to outright speed, the Dutch and to some extent the Belgians are among the fastest in the world. They may lack other abilities, like climbing strength, but at that one speciality they're superb.

If all races in Britain were like they are in Holland — where only a handful of so-called classics follow the British pattern of long courses — you'd get most of the speed work you need in the races themselves. But even there they're starting to recognise that competition alone isn't the be-all and end-all of training.

The clue to speed in races lies both in how fast you touch in your training sprints, and in the time it takes you to recover. If you can sprint — jump clear — in a road race and then sprint again before anyone else has recovered, you'll be clear of the bunch. And, as we've seen, once you're clear you don't need to go any faster than those chasing you. You only have to match their pace and you'll stay clear. That's a point any time triallist knows well.

It could be that it takes you half a dozen attempts to get clear. But each attempt weakens the opposition who, because of your training, will take longer to recover. If you can achieve that kind of superiority, it'll be you who controls the race. You'll decide when to attack, whether to take others with you or to go it alone. And if you do take others with you, you can decide where to axe them before the line. You will decide and dictate and you will win.

It all comes from absolute speed in training, and absolute speed can be a vomit-inducing experience. Small wonder that so many aren't willing to go the whole way.

Strength

There was an old Greek, years ago, who decided to win a bet. His mate had told him he'd not be able to lift a fully-grown bull above his head by the end of the year.

Well, no sportsman will turn down a good challenge, and the Greeks are a philosophical lot. Our hero worked out how to do it. And instead of trying to lift the big bull straightaway, he started lifting a young bull instead. Every day the young bull grew just that little bit heavier, but every day the Greek's muscles became that little bit stronger, and each time he managed to lift the growing bull. By the end of the year it was a really big creature, but the Greek's muscles had developed as well and when the day came he won his bet with ease.

Good climbers have high power-to-weight ratio. Robert Millar's a good example – plenty of power and lightly built.

Do you recognise the overload principle in all this? Do you recognise the progression and the specificity of the training?

You need strength whenever you move your own weight, let alone a bull's as well. Isaac Newton, like me, lived in Lincolnshire. He worked out the laws of motion, whereby a weight will move in the same direction at the same speed unless there's a resistance to prevent it. On a bike, the resistance comes from the air, the wind, the road, and just a little bit from the bike's bearings. The resistance grows much greater on a hill. Therefore the rider needs strength to overcome all that. And you need still more to accelerate – the greater the acceleration, the greater the strength needed.

Strength doesn't necessarily mean big muscles, although big muscles are usually stronger than skinny ones. But even a skinny muscle can get three times stronger without getting bigger. And skinny bike riders sometimes don't need to be as strong as 13-stone giants simply because they have less weight to propel in the first place.

The important factor is your strength-to-weight ratio, and it explains why the best hill-climbers are usually weedy blokes and the best sprinters are giant hulks, often with a trace of surplus body fat.

Don't ask me why a muscle gets stronger with work. I don't know. Nor does anyone, truthfully. But work harder than you've done before and you'll get stronger. If you can't get the loan of a bull, do it by weight-training, which you can control. The way your strength increases will startle you.

There is, actually, a technical difference between strength and power which needs explaining. Strength is what you need to move a weight once, like Olympic weightlifters. Power, which is what bike riders need, is the ability to lift smaller weights repeatedly – for lift, read press (as in pedals). So power is a combination of strength and stamina. The two words get confused all the time, so I may as well warn you now that it is quite likely to happen in this book. Sorry.

The whole idea of strength or power training came to cycling later than many other sports. Swimmers and runners cottoned on years before. A chap called Vaughan Thomas, a top-class physiologist who's done a lot of work with bike riders, has written a book called *Science and Sport*, which is a pretty good read. He looks back to the days when weight-training was unknown:

When I came to analyse a survey conducted among top-class racing cyclists in 1965, I found that the most common answer to the question on strength development was 'The cyclist does not need strength, only suppleness.' Well, a jelly has no strength and plenty of suppleness, but I can hardly visualise it winning the Tour de France!

This very popular misconception was one of the things that convinced me that a drastic re-education was needed in many aspects of sport.

Psychology

The trouble with bike racing is that, initially, it's a pretty good feeling dressing up in all those flashy clothes. You've only got to see how quick bike riders are to follow the latest clothing fashion to realise that. The disadvantage is that the feeling of anti-climax and uselessness is all the greater when you get dropped, or passed in a time trial by someone who started 20 minutes behind you.

I wonder where Norman Sheil is now. He reckoned that in every road race field of 40 (there were only 40 riders in a road race in those days, but don't let that bother you), there were only ten who expected to win. They'd trained hard and with purpose. They'd make the crucial moves and figure in the final break.

Another ten were racing but didn't have the attitude or preparation to succeed, except by chance. They *hoped* to win, but they didn't *expect* to win. As such, they were genuinely racing but without any real chance of success.

The next ten weren't racing at all, although they fiercely believed they were. They were the ones who'd be secretly relieved when the first 20 cleared off up the road and left them to settle down to reach the line at their own pace. I think I was in this group when I was racing. We usually beat the last ten, but only because they'd been shot off in the first two laps.

You can persuade yourself that the impossible is quite possible. Just think how double-glazing salesmen have to psyche themselves up. Or door-to-door floggers of life insurance. They go on high-powered sales courses that make them firmly convinced they can succeed. You've got this book and all your wonderful training. Just think of the possibilities!

3 Of fatties and thinnies

Not everyone can become a racing cyclist. Or, if they do, they could be at a disadvantage. It's all a question of somatotypes, you see.

Somatotyping is a way of classifying body shapes. There are three basic types:

endomorphic, a soft roundness in the body;
mesomorphic, a tendency to muscularity; and
ectomorphic, lightly-built skinniness.

You score from one to seven in each category – because few people fit only one category – but obviously if you score highly in one class you have to score less in the other two.

It's probably easier to understand if you draw a triangle with slightly bulging sides. The left-hand corner is endomorphy (tubbiness), the right-hand corner is ectomorphy (skinniness), and the top is mesomorphy (muscularity). Each corner is obviously an extreme.

A theoretically average person would score 4–4–4 and end up right in the middle of the triangle, an exact mix of tubbiness, skinniness and muscularity. In fact, any group of non-athletes will pretty much fill the triangle, with a concentration towards the centre.

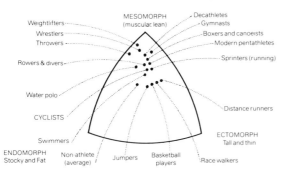

Fig. 2 *Somatotype of male Olympic competitors*

Cyclists and other athletes are so widely studied – not least at the Olympic Games, which is an orgy of weighing and measuring and a physiologist's delight – that it's easy to plot where each sport will fall.

As you'd expect, athletes in general fill the top right-hand third of the triangle. There are no fatties, but they range all the way from the very muscular to just short of outright thinness. Most are between the edge and the middle of the triangle, which means most athletes have muscles and no great tendency to fatness, but they're heavily-built or fairly thin according to their sport.

The average cyclist is about a third the way in from the right-hand edge and a third down from the muscular top. Boxers, canoeists, gymnasts and decathletes tend to be more muscular. Swimmers, distance runners, race walkers and basketball players tend to be thinner and more lightly-muscled.

On the other hand, weight-lifters, throwers and wrestlers have heavier builds and (lifters especially) more muscles, but only a fractionally greater tendency towards fatness.

No more than you might expect, you think. But size comes into it as well. Most Olympic cyclists are shorter than you might think. The average height for short-distance runners, for example, is six feet. Then the list descends through middle and long-distance running, race walking and jumping, right through another ten sports before it reaches cyclists – who are just less than five feet nine inches, or much the average height of the rest of the population. Their average weight is 68.9 kg, but they have some of the least body fat of all sports – $2\frac{1}{2}$ per cent, along with cross-country skiers and long-distance runners, compared to 15 per cent in the (national) average male, or 25 per cent for the average woman. The average for male athletes of all types is 7.5 per cent for men and 12 per cent for women.

But if that sort of physical selection decides who – so far as statistics are concerned – will make a good bike rider, what decides who will make a long-distance time triallist and who a track sprinter?

Well, obviously physical build is again a factor. Track sprinting is a power and strength sport, so a sprinter's build tends towards that of a weight-thrower. Time triallists are primarily distance competitors so, even allowing for the power they need, their build is more like that of a marathon runner. But is there more? Yes there is.

Muscles are made of tiny fibres grouped in bundles. When the nerves carry an electrical signal to the relevant muscle from the brain, the bundles contract and creep over each other, shortening the muscle. This action extends the joint so that the muscle can take the shortest line, and the straightening limb – the leg, in this instance – pushes against the pedal. Muscles always pull; it is the limb that pushes.

Now, not all the muscle bundles fire off at the same time. If they did so, the power of the contraction would be too great for the joint and your leg would break at the knee. Also, if all the bundles — or even most of them — worked at the same time, your movements would be very clumsy and jerky.

That's why the most delicate muscles — e.g. in your eye — have a higher ratio of nerves to muscle bundles than, say, your legs, which are very much stronger but are unable to make delicate movements.

The number of bundles triggered off at a time depends on the power of the electrical charge through the nerves. The more urgent the instruction from the brain, the greater the charge. At the lowest charges, only a few bundles contract; at progressively higher levels of instruction, more and more bundles shorten and thus provide stronger muscle movements.

Many people believe that training — local muscular endurance — can raise the sensitivity of bundles, so that more will work at one time. But if that happens, the greater muscular work will produce increased fatigue, so there has to be a control.

This is provided by the different types of fibre that make up the bundles. Red fibres have a lot of myoglobin, a protein which stores oxygen. That makes it an aerobic fibre which will work steadily for long periods for so long as oxygen is available to it. A red fibre takes a tenth of a second to tighten up completely, which makes it a slow-twitch fibre.

Fast-twitch fibres, on the other hand, have less myoglobin and appear paler. This type of fibre takes only a fifth of the red fibre's time to shorten, but it tires more quickly. However, to compensate for this, it's pretty good at working anaerobically and turns out a lot of very hard work in a short period.

Training will make both types of fibres work more efficiently, but you can't change the proportions of each. In other words, you're born either fast-twitch or slow-twitch.

Sprinters clearly need to have a large proportion of fast-twitch fibres, which weight and sprint training will develop further.

Leaving aside road racing for a moment, because tactics and pace-taking distort the picture, longer races need as much as 80 per cent of slow-twitch fibres. But remember that although a larger percentage of slow-twitch fibres will increase your staying power, they'll do nothing for your acceleration. So it's no coincidence that track riders, roadmen and time triallists are so characteristically different in style and character.

The joys of victory. Beppe Saronni wins Milan-San Remo. It's all a matter of oxygen uptake, power and body type – and talent comes into it as well.

Unfortunately, there's no sure way of knowing in which group you fall without having a sliver cut out of yourself. But, as any boffin will inform you, science doesn't always tell us something new; it just explains what we'd already suspected. So the chances are that if you've been riding for more than a year or two, you know instinctively if you're more suited to being a sprinter or a 24-hour man. If you can cope with all but the extremes, it suggests you have a middle-of-the-road twitch make-up.

It would be a sad thing, though, if you specialised too severely or too early. I don't believe any rider should specialise in road or track or time-trialling before he becomes a senior at 18. Under-18s are apprentices learning their craft. And those over 18 should have an occasional stab at something different to provide both a mental break and a change of training.

How the bulk of that training is made up will depend on what you're asking from it. Training, remember, is specific to the activity.

In the list given here, take 1 as strength, 2 as speed, 3 as stamina, and 4 as skill. I'm assuming you need psychology for all branches of cycling.

The list shows the main need at the top, running down in order of decreasing importance.

Sprint	12-hour	Hill-climb		25-miles		Road racing
		short	long	gears	fixed	
1	3	1	1	4	4	All,
2	1	4	4	1	2	in
4	4	2	3	2	3	any
3	2	3	2	3	1	order

The foregoing is a list supplied to candidates on courses run by the British Cycling Coaching Scheme. Another list, drawn up by Dr Gerard Daniëls of Belgium, gives the following information:

Track riders

Sprint   Exceptional thigh strength
              Exceptional co-ordination
              Little stamina
              Little recovery

Pursuit   Exceptional stamina
              Very good recovery
              Normal muscle power
              Normal co-ordination

Road riders

Distance   Exceptional stamina
(e.g. classics) Very good recovery
              Powerful thigh muscle
              Normal co-ordination

Most riders reach their peak at around 27. Joop Zoetemelk, though, was closer to 40 when he won his only world championship in 1985.

Hill climbers*   Very good stamina
Very good recovery
Very good co-ordination
Normal muscle strength

(* If the requirements here strike you as odd, when you compare them to the BCCS list, bear in mind that in flat Flanders, hill-climbers aren't enthusiasts who sprint up short hills in the Chilterns. They're people like Lucien van Impe who go wheeling over mountain passes in the Tour de France.)

On the face of it, we have precious little choice about which bit of cycling we're going to be good at. And just to depress you further, there's also the question of age. Olympic medal winners have been as young as seven years and as old as 72. The average age of Olympic competitors as a whole is 24 for men and 20 for women. After 25, your physical capacity falls off by a hundredth every year, so you're at only 75 per cent of your peak level by the time you're 50.

Cycling fits that pattern almost exactly. The average age for Olympic riders is 23.6 for men, younger than middle-distance runners (24.9), marathon runners (25.9) and shooters (37.8), but older by far than swimmers (19.2 for men and 16.3 for women).

More than 80 per cent of all Olympic medallists are less than 30 years old and just 15 per cent between 30 and 42.

Now, it doesn't hold with every sport, but in cycling it certainly seems true: the older a competitor becomes, the more chance there is that he'll be involved in an endurance sport. Talents like Reg Harris, who made a comeback in professional sprinting when he was old enough to be his rivals' father, are rare indeed. Time trials of 50 miles and more attract more and more veterans (in this country, age 40 and upwards). And although there is a veteran class in road racing, it's small indeed compared to its counterpart in time trialling.

Skill starts to count more as age increases, and many a wise head has compensated for old legs. Raymond Poulidor was still racing successfully in top-class road racing on his 40th birthday, for example. Many veteran time triallists produce faster times than they did in their youth, a combination of better roads, better equipment and more experience. But in the end, age starts to tell and the veteran time trialling association has a handicapping system.

Strength and mobility vary according to age, too. Young riders are restricted to low gears which they have to turn fast. Their co-ordination is greater than their strength. With older riders it can be the other way round.

Fortunately, cycling is a perfect sport for those who are growing older. A study in 1965, covering 27 sports, found only three sports commonly practised by 75-year-olds, one of them cycling. And, for your own amusement, here's a table produced at the turn of the century by a chap who made a study of 400 Czechoslovakian athletes. It looks like pretty good news for bike riders, if one studies the average age at which each group died.

Sport	Number studied	Average age at death
Cycling	54	65
Gymnastics	122	59
Rowing	17	55
Swimming	6	54
Athletics	61	53
Football	116	51
Tennis	7	51
Marathon	17	47

But then, that was Czechoslovakia at the turn of the century!

4 An end to anti-training

We all differ, but generally you lose fitness at a slightly slower pace than you gained it. And it takes time to regain it once more.

In the old days, bike riders argued that their bodies were under such stress all through the racing season that they needed a break during the winter. This attitude was helped along magnificently by the old style of club life. Now, so far as I'm concerned, it's nothing but a shame that cycling's not the sociable sport that it once was. But equally, the change in styles means that the old all-or-nothing approach is, thankfully, something of the past.

If cycling clubs have ceased to be winter drinking clubs, it's only because in most cases they're much more interested in athletic performance. Some sort of break's still important, but it's a break within limits, a break that still includes cycling if not necessarily cycle racing.

One activity in the off-season which is not only physiologically valuable but mentally refreshing (and saves you riding alone on the darkest and iciest of winter roads) is pleasure riding.

Assuming for the moment that racing stops for you in October — that you won't be riding cyclo-cross in the winter — then the last months of the year can be for pleasure riding. It's a time to remember that cycling's really a very friendly sport to be enjoyed with some of the funniest, most amusing people in the world. It's all too easy to forget this side of the sport, if you let life become a succession of training, loading roof racks, racing and re-loading the roof rack.

Get out on club runs, go youth hostelling, just go for rides to look at all the countryside you've not noticed previously. It's a long-term investment. You might not want to race all your life; heaven's above . . . you may get married and have kids and just not have the time! Learn to get a different kind of fun from cycling and discover an activity you can carry on all your life.

We do everything best when it's a novelty, and unless you give yourself a break you won't approach the next season in the right frame of mind. So many riders become stale because, although they don't realise it, they've got fed up with the continual round of training and racing. It all becomes a chore, a duty, rather than a real pleasure. And although you may still enjoy it, you don't put the same effort and enthusiasm into it because there's no contrast, no difference.

Sharing your time between cycling and another sport is also a good idea, for several reasons. For a start, the weather's often too bad or too miserable to ride as much as you would like. Second, a different sport develops you in other directions. And third, most cyclists are dreadfully immobile and uncoordinated and almost any other sport is good news.

There's no greater bore in life than the cyclist who can talk about absolutely nothing else but his sport. Surely you must have suffered from him as well? The sad but inevitable result is that you go off the bore and the bore goes off cycling, because even bores get bored in the end.

The choice of an alternative sport is entirely up to you – take your pick from anything the local council offers at evening classes. But my personal advice is to avoid football and rugby. There's a completely different aura and attitude to them from those to cycling, and a greater chance of injury. The other ball sports, though, are great. Take every chance to play basketball (if you're tall enough) and volleyball. They're both indoor and no-contact sports.

Here's a list that Gerard Daniëls drew up:

Athletics	sprinting – muscle power and co-ordination
	mid-distance – recovery
	distance – stamina
	jumping – muscle power and co-ordination
	throwing – muscle power
Badminton	co-ordination
Basketball	co-ordination and a little muscle power
Boxing	co-ordination and muscle power
Handball	muscle power and co-ordination
Hockey	stamina
Judo	muscle power and co-ordination
Canoeing	endurance

Rowing	short-distance – muscle power
	long-distance – stamina and recovery
Rugby	muscle power and stamina
Table tennis	co-ordination
Tennis	muscle power and co-ordination
Gymnastics	strength and co-ordination
Football	outdoor – strength and stamina
	indoor – co-ordination
Volleyball	muscle power and co-ordination
Water polo	muscle power and stamina
Wrestling	muscle power
Swimming	short-distance – muscle power
	mid-distance – recovery
	long-distance – stamina and recovery
	diving – co-ordination

Your own personal tastes and needs are like nobody else's. All I can say is that I have met very few cyclists who are sufficiently mobile to touch their toes comfortably, let alone as nimble as gymnasts and runners. Nor do they ever seem as co-ordinated. In fact, watching cyclists run round obstacles is almost comical at times, so look for a winter activity that'll combine a fair bit of twisting and turning with something producing co-ordination.

There's a growing trend towards circuit training, too, increasingly at special classes for bikies. Circuit training, done properly, is a wonderful system for stressing every part of the body in turn. That means your heart and lungs carry on working hard even though your legs, arms, back, stomach and so on all get tired one after the other.

In a perfect world, the best idea would be to combine circuit training, casual cycling, weight training and an alternative sport, all in the same week. That's in a perfect world. On the other hand, you may well want some time to yourself. Not everyone is as devoted or dotty as training manuals suggest.

The trouble is that it's hard to select one alternative activity in preference to all the others that are available but come what may you have to carry on cycling or there'll be no crossover effect.

The most beneficial activity is certainly circuit training, because it does everything you could possibly want from it. But then, it's not always wonderfully exciting.

A good circuit training class lasts about an hour to an hour and a half. One of the best I've experienced started with gentle running round the gym, moved on to mobility training (stretching, twisting, all that sort of thing), then went on to the circuit itself before ending with a very informal game of basketball. At the end, you certainly knew you'd done it.

When someone asked Norman Sheil whether it was worthwhile, he said:

> If you mean 'Does it make me go faster?' then the answer is no. If you mean 'Does it make me fitter?' then the answer is yes.
>
> Circuit training does not make you a better bike rider. It is an exercise to develop the heart and lungs, and because of this you are more able to handle hard cycle racing when the time comes. Unfortunately, too many riders feel that the work they have done in the winter has no bearing on their fitness during the summer. Yet when you question them, you find that they have achieved a higher degree of fitness which not only comes quicker but is longer lasting.

Sheil went on to say that a rider who neglects circuit training finds later that his fitness is patchy and, although he may race well at the start of the year, other apparently stronger riders overtake him when the season-proper gets under way. The great thing about circuit training is that it not only builds stamina and a firm base for later, more advanced training, it gives you the ability to suffer. Oh golly, yes. It certainly makes you able to suffer.

Circuit training started in the early 1950s and the credit goes to two physical education teachers at Leeds University. Until then, gym training had always been the kind of organised exercises that great numbers of Germans still seem to enjoy on the beach each summer. Swedish gymnastics it was called. I don't know why.

Anyway, they set out a circle of exercises. They are deliberately very easy exercises to understand, because it's important that the skill factor of each exercise is very low and that each one takes as little time as possible to learn. They might be low-resistance exercises like jumping, which will produce stamina and a little muscular power, or power exercises working against a resistance, like lifting a bench or some other weight.

An arm exercise doesn't follow an arm exercise, or a leg exercise follow a leg exercise. The sequence is such that the agony is spread round the body evenly and muscles etc. are worked in turn. A typical circle might be: jumping to touch a spot high on the wall; press-ups; skipping; chin-ups (pulling your weight up to a beam); back extensions (lying on your front and lifting your outstretched legs, thereby extending your back); trunk curls; shuttle running; sit-ups.

That's just one circuit thought up at random. You can have any number of others, all based on the sport concerned, on overall fitness, or on what you think are your special needs. Progression is by increasing the number of repetitions of each exercise; increasing the number to be carried out in a set time; reducing the rest time between each exercise; increasing the number of circuits, and so on. The method varies according to the way the class is conducted.

You can obtain details of your nearest specialist class by contacting the British Cycling Federation. Also, the weekly magazine *Cycling* often carries a list in the autumn.

What you get out of those classes depends entirely on what you put in — it's like any other training. The problem is that as the circuit intensifies, so there's a temptation to clip some of the exercises so that they take less time. If the coach suddenly requires you to do eight sit-ups in the time you previously did five, the natural temptation is to do less of a sit-up, or a much sloppier one. This, if the coach doesn't realise what is happening, means that the circuit will be tightened up even further, so that your sit-ups, star jumps, bench presses or whatever become flabbier and flabbier. Before too long you're not only deluding yourself, you're actually getting no benefit either. And as others in the class notice the 'progress' you're apparently making, they start cutting corners as well. The whole thing becomes a farce.

If you can't get to a class, it's possible (although not easy) to devise your own circuit at home. At one time I recommended it. Since then, practical experience has shown that the rest of the family take a dim view of crashes and groans from your bedroom while they're downstairs watching Terry Wogan. And strengthening your leg muscles by jumping up the stairs two at a time is often seen as anti-social and excessively wearing on the stair carpet. Much better, I think, to play another sport instead.

Why not try running? After all, there's no more natural activity. But don't overdo it all of a sudden or you'll ache like crazy for days afterwards. What happens, you see, is that the hamstrings at the back of your legs get shorter because they never stretch fully as you ride. That's the body adapting to the very curious pedalling position you've forced on it. But tight muscles are both inefficient and sometimes painful to try and get back to their proper length.

Running *will* do it, and it'll probably also raise your heart and lung rate higher than all but the hardest cycling. And, like all other non-cycling activities, a lot of the fitness benefits will transfer directly to the bike provided you keep cycling all through the winter.

This question of muscles getting shorter — or, sometimes, longer —

because of cycling is an important one. Apart from anything else, it makes you look a mess. Just have a look at the pictures in cycling magazines of the Fifties. Or just occasionally, watch the long-distance veterans shuffling across the floor at the British Best All-rounder prize-giving. They're a bunch of stooping men with rounded shoulders, funny walks and necks sticking forward at 45 degrees. They look like question marks on the move. They don't look like any other athletes I've ever seen.

This mobility business – fluidity, range of movement – worries a lot of coaches. The late Peter Valentine went as far as saying that many cyclists are spastic, which, in the sporting if not the pathological sense, they probably are. They simply cannot move their bodies, their limbs, as far as they ought to be able to, in each direction.

Stretched or shortened muscles are part of the overloading effect – but not a good one. Stretched back muscles require more energy, more contraction than normal in order to support the back. The result: backache. Now, don't get me wrong; there are many more causes of backache than over-stretched spinal muscles. But if you're looking for a cause, it's a pretty good place to start.

Every joint is worked by two (or more) muscles – one to bend it, the other to straighten it. Most sports, cycling included, use one more than the other. The straightening may be done against a resistance (as in pedalling) and the bending against less hindrance. The result, when one muscle is taut and the other stretched or of normal length, is an imbalance and a fall-off in power, as the joint is no longer able to work over its complete range.

Fortunately, stretching muscles back to their proper length (which may be longer than you suspected) is pretty straightforward. Just take it steady and stretch.

Don't, though, do what you may have been taught at school. Don't bob up and down until you can eventually touch your toes, as I was taught. There are still a few teachers somewhere who do things this way, but it seems obvious to me that if you jerk a muscle you risk tearing or straining it. Sadly, I didn't realise it *then* and we bobbed and jerked, and did bunny hops and other potentially dangerous exercises, and hobbled about in pain afterwards. But in those days it was all part of Growing Up to be A Man.

Stretching exercises these days are yoga-like movements, done slowly and gently, yet still with pressure.

Sudden movements, like dropping down sharply from the waist to touch your toes, produce strange reactions in your muscles. In toe-touching, for example, the rear thigh muscles slacken right off in order to let you bob downwards. But then it's almost as though they sense something is about to happen. They suddenly tighten up at the last moment as if they're defending themselves. It happens at the wrong moment; just as they're tightening, so your body weight falls to its lowest and gives the muscle a hefty twang. The result is a collection of neatly-torn fibres that fill with blood and make the rest of the week a miserable experience.

Just think what ten minutes a day of gentle yoga and stretching can do for you. Look at what Richard Hittleman reckoned on telly, anyway: 'Another way to use the power which will be made available to you through yoga exercises is to project this force throughout the entire world with the thought of harmony and peace behind it.'

I never saw a lot of harmony in the sweating bikies I saw collapsing on the floor of my gym, but perhaps I didn't take it seriously enough.

Pick the exercises you want from the following selection; do two or three a day and make sure that you've done them all in the course of a week.

Cobra

Lie face downward on the floor with your feet together and your hands beneath your chin, palms down. Press down with your hands as you would for a press-up, but bend from the small of your back, keeping your hips on the floor. Crane your neck backwards to look as far up and behind you as you can. Hold for five seconds, then relax. Repeat ten times.

Alternate leg pulls

Sit on the floor with both legs spread wide in front. Place your hands palm down on the top of your right thigh, keeping your thumbs together. Slowly, without bobbing, push your hands down towards your ankle. If you can, grasp the sole of your shoe without bending your leg, and hold it for ten seconds. Then relax. Repeat five times with each leg.

Side bend

Stand upright with your feet at shoulder width and your arms outstretched at each side of you. Slowly bend sideways from the waist to your left, bring your right arm upright, and push down the outside of your left thigh with your left hand. Push as far down as you can without bobbing. Come up slowly and repeat on the other side. Repeat five times each side.

Roll twist

Stand upright with your hands on your hips and your feet at shoulder width. Bend from your hips and, keeping your legs straight, draw as wide a circle with your head as you can, bending as far as possible forwards, sideways and back. As with all exercises, do it slowly, then stop and repeat in the other direction.

Standing twist

Stand upright with your feet together and your arms held out in front of you with the thumbs together. Slowly twist to the left as far as you can, finishing the turn by coming up on tiptoe. You should be able to point your arms nearly directly behind you. Then come back slowly and twist the other way.

Arm and leg stretch

Stand upright, legs together and one arm pointing straight upwards. Reach back with your other arm and grasp your ankle (your leg should be brought up behind you – sorry, didn't I tell you that?) Pull your foot upwards and back and stretch up with your upright arm. Relax and repeat on the other side.

Hip extensions

Lie face down on the floor with your arms beside you. Push down hard with your hands and raise your legs, keeping your ankles together. Don't raise your head. Repeat four times.

Yoga bow

Lie face down with your legs curled up behind you. Reach back and grasp your ankles. Raising your head and arching your back, pull to rock forwards and backwards on your stomach.

Plough

Lie on your back with your arms alongside you and your feet together. Slowly raise your straight legs to the vertical. Push down hard on the ground with your palms and let your legs fall slowly down behind your head. Keeping your legs straight, touch the floor with your toes, then bring your knees in to touch your forehead. Gently uncurl into the lying position. Repeat six times.

Hip bend

Stand upright with your feet together and your arms held upright. Bend as far as you can to your left, come up again, then bend to the right. Bend five times in each direction.

Rishi

Stand upright with your feet slightly apart. Bend slowly at the waist and grasp your left ankle with your right hand. Keep your left arm straight and, still holding your ankle, twist as far round to the left as you can. Repeat in the opposite direction.

Calf stretch

Stand upright with your feet together and toes pointing forward at an arm's length plus six inches from a wall. Fall forward to place your palms on the wall at shoulder height. Keeping your back straight, your bottom tucked in and your heels firmly on the floor, bend slowly from the elbows until your elbows are touching the wall. Hold for a minute.

Leg clasp

Slowly bend forward as if to touch your toes, but clasp your hands instead behind your calves. Slowly pull with your arms until eventually you can touch your knees with your forehead. Try three times.

Leg cross

Lie on the floor on your back with your legs together and arms at your sides. Move your arms out sideways just enough to keep your balance and lift one leg as straight and high as you can. Slowly bring it across your body, keeping it straight and your shoulders on the floor, and touch the ground with your toe. Relax and repeat with the other leg.

If you regard all this as yoga, you have to think beautiful thoughts. If you think it's just plain exercise, you're allowed to swear a bit.

5 Muscles and men

The other things you've got to keep your eye on all through the off-season are your power and strength – your muscles. This can be complicated. For one thing, the bits and pieces you need might not be available. For another, the kind of weight training that one sport needs isn't the same as another. Let me explain.

My Aunt Nelly thinks weight training makes you look like Geoff Capes which, to her, is no bad thing. She fancies men with beards and she goes for hunks who can pull ships across Rotterdam harbour and park Long Vehicles with a length of rope. That's the impression most people have, or else they think it's all a matter of pumping up your muscles, rubbing on some oil and posing for the kind of magazines that seem to be published mainly in America.

You can do that if you want. Who am I to deny you the fun of kicking sand in the face of seven-stone weaklings? All I'm saying is that Aunt Nelly would never see why muscle-pumping won't help you win bike races when it apparently does so much for big Geoff Capes.

Go back to when we were on about power and strength.

'Strength . . .', these are the words of Al Murray, whose name has been whispered with hallowed respect in weight-training circles . . . 'Strength is the ability to lift a weight without the help of momentum, speed or technique.' In other words, you go very red in the face, shout something very loudly, and heave something heavy up above your head and hold it there until the judges say you can put it down again. Or until you drop it.

That's not power, though. Power is what you need for cycling. You need to be able to move smallish weights over and over again – as in pedalling. Muscle-men can move massive weights that mere mortals and wimps can't imagine. But they can't repeat it without a helluva rest. In your style of weight training, you'll be moving weights repeatedly – up to maybe thirty times.

There does have to be an optimum weight, though. If it's too light, all you get is endurance. Local muscular endurance, to be exact. As you increase the weight and decrease the number of lifts – the repetitions – so the effect differs.

On a sliding scale, it goes like this:

ENDURANCE – ENDURANCE AND POWER – POWER – POWER AND STRENGTH – STRENGTH – RUPTURE

There's some overlap, of course. And as you improve, so the weights increase. The principle of overload again. Remember?

The doctor who's been looking after the American amateurs during their bewildering rise to world status is a chap called Ed Burke. He says:

The philosophy of many coaches and riders . . . is that resistance training will stifle the smooth motion of the legs, add excess body weight, and work against the suppleness needed to spin at 90 rpm or faster. However, I believe that proper strength training will improve any athlete – male or female, young or old. The better a cyclist is, the more he or she can gain from proper strength training. You will become faster, more flexible, have more endurance, and be less susceptible to injury.

And here, I rush to point out, Ed Burke uses the words 'strength training' in their most general terms. For strength training, read 'power training'.

Even so, there have obviously been non-believers.

Some world-class cyclists and coaches have stated that they never use resistance training in their programmes. But consider that almost all outstanding cyclists are blessed with superior neurological and physiological systems. To this, add cardiovascular endurance training, skill and race experience, and the performance level becomes far above average . . . even when strength and power may be only average.

I think that without exception, strength training is mandatory for these and all other cyclists to reach their full potential.

Thank you, Doctor. In other words, they were pretty hot stuff already, but with weight training they'd be even better.

Of course, the trouble with weight training is that you need all the mullarkey that goes with it. All the weights, and bars, and dumbbells and so on. You can club together with your mates and buy a set, of course. You do still sometimes find them in *Exchange and Mart*. But even when you've got them, you still need somewhere to use them. You need a lot of space, especially if using a garage. Nothing is more disconcerting during a bench press than to have a pile of punctured tubs descend on you. Except, perhaps, a rusty pram or a lawn mower.

Of course, weight training is bad news for people who live in flats, particularly those who live *below* where it is taking place.

Considering all the problems – the equipment, the schedule, techniques and safety drawbacks – it really is much better to go to an organised gym. Some of the coaches who run circuit training organise weight training as well.

A lot of coaches stick to the traditional bars and weights like you see on the telly. They're cheaper, they're portable, and they're easier if you've got several people training together. But some instructors have taken high-technology under their wing and got these wonderful Multi-gym and Nautilus machines. You've probably seen them: they look like a cube of scaffolding pipes with various levers and ropes and a pile of central weights shaped like loaves.

Both types can be very dangerous if you let enthusiasm get the better of sense, but the machinery is – as you might expect from something so very much more expensive – more flexible. But apart from technical differences, the principles remain the same for both.

Never be tempted into racing or competition in a weight-training gym. The important thing is not how much you and your mate can lift but how much you've improved since your last visit. He will certainly be a different shape from you, so that all the weights and levers are different. And his needs may be very different as well, so there's no comparison. Exactly similar routines may produce varying results in different riders. In a bench press, for example, the effect will be different for a man with a large chest from that for a chap of lighter build.

What's more, the fact that someone can lift more than you – or tug or press, or whatever – doesn't mean he'll be a better climber or sprinter. You could have a better power-to-body-weight ratio.

A good coach recognises all these points. He may even set you off on a routine for a cramped chest rather than throw you straight into general power training. Weight training has great remedial value.

There's another point, too. There are certain exercises you should avoid if you're about 23 or younger. It's all to do with your spine. The exact age at which your spine hardens varies. But until it does, it's a bit like a green stick. Put a heavy weight on it and it'll bend out of shape.

A developed adult can hold surprisingly heavy weights on his spine with no real damage. On the other hand, you could run into trouble later in life if you try to do the same while a teenager.

As Norman Sheil says:

Strength training with weights should be given careful consideration when it is applied to the schoolboy rider. Natural development is very important to the young and this should never be interfered with in any way, so light weights should be the rule at all times, as this will not affect normal growth but will enable the rider to develop the skill and technique of weight training.

Then, when he is older and able to increase the weight that he uses, he will be able to carry out the exercises in the proper manner and will be aware of what this type of training entails.

6 Men and muscles

Now look – you've got to make me a promise. I'm just an ordinary sort of bloke and I can do without lawyers coming round with posh briefcases and heavy writs wrapped up in red ribbon. Let's get it straight right from the start that weights are potentially dangerous and that you need someone to show you how. I can give you a start, but really you need a coach.

What's more, you can do all sorts of damage to yourself by cutting corners, by racing, by lifting too much, or by lifting when you're cold. I don't suppose it's any more dangerous than road racing, but you *know* about that. Weights are probably still a mystery. Just remember one thing – Geoff Capes didn't get to be the world's strongest man by rupturing himself along the way.

Whether you use olde-worlde weights or one of those new-fangled pieces of gym machinery, the first bit is the same. You've got to warm up. Not just the odd skip – spend a good ten minutes at it, running, jumping, swinging on things, turning head-over-heels. Get the blood flowing, get your joints mobile, get your muscles loose and floppy. (Or were loose and floppy muscles part of the problem in the first place?)

If you use a gym machine, we now part company because there are several different sorts and you can't do all exercises on all machines. What I describe next may well adapt, though, but do seek advice.

First of all make sure you've got no flapping clothing and that no muscle-bound beachboy's likely to fling a medicine ball playfully in your direction. Beware projecting bits of furniture. And wear firm shoes – even outdoor shoes if necessary – rather than plimsolls.

Get hold of the bar and slip a 20 lb disc on each end. If you've gone metric, just halve the numbers and call them kilograms – a 20 lb disc is much the same as a 10 kg one. The weights are held in place by collars. If you don't use them, the weights fall off the end and drop on your feet, so they're important. There'll also be some method of stopping the discs sliding inwards, thereby making you lose balance and sending the whole caboodle over your neighbour's feet. However they work, the collars must be there and they must be very firmly tightened.

Practise picking up the weighted bar and putting it down again. Just that. Walk up to it, stand with your shoelaces under the bar and your feet about shoulder-width apart. Keep your head up (stare straight ahead) and your shoulders back. Bend your knees and let your straightened arms drop down outside your legs until they reach the bar. Grasp it in an overhand grip (in other words, with your knuckles pointing forward).

Fig. 3 Lifting the bar

Straighten your knees and stand up. Remember: no bending the arms, no looking down, no pushing your shoulders forward.

Try it a few times. Up, down, up, down. Then try the first exercise in any weight-training schedule.

High pull

With the same weights on the bar, address the bar (a posh way of saying walk up to it and stand with your feet under it as I've described) and grab hold of it as you did before. But instead of just lifting it to thigh height, continue the lift so that you end up with the bar at eyebrow height and your elbows sticking out to the side. (*Don't* flick your hands back towards you to support the bar like you see on telly; your thumbs should be pointing downwards all the time.) At the same time, go up on tiptoe.

Now lower the bar to thigh height again. Come back off tip-toe, bend your knees and lower the bar to the floor. Make it a swift, smooth action, up and down, but don't cut corners.

You do this 20 times straight off at the start of any weight training session (and it makes you red in the face).

The number of times you lift a weight without a rest is called the *repetition*. The high pulls in the warming-up session are therefore 20 repetitions, or reps. If you had a brief rest and then did another 20, you'd have done two *sets* of 20 *repetitions*. OK on the terminology?

High pulls are always done with a light weight because they're just for warming up. However, all the other exercises have enough weight to produce greater power (overloading) but not so much that you simply grind to a halt.

The weight you use should be decided by trial and error. Ideally, you should be able to lift it two and a half sets and no more before you start struggling. Put it down immediately you struggle or have to twist and wriggle to get the weight to move. That's when injuries happen. The weight is obviously too heavy if you are unable to complete two sets (you'll see the number of reps in the schedules that come later) and too light if you can complete all three.

The routine is this: find the weight for each exercise with which you can manage two and a half sets. Carry on with that weight until you can manage the full number of sets without undue struggling – and by that I don't count the usual red-in-the-face-and-muttered-oaths act, but the kind of struggling where you're clearly getting away from the safe, textbook style.

Fig. 4 High pull (lift the bar to eyebrow height)

When you can do the specified number of sets, add 5 lb in the case of arm exercises, dorsal hyperextensions and sit-ups, or 10 lb for leg and back exercises. That should put you back somewhere in the two-and-a-half-sets range. You carry on once more until you manage all three sets. This is the principle of overload and overadjustment coming into play.

Keep an accurate note of the reps and weight you managed, and the dates. Remember that you'll lift less if you're feeling tired or if the weather's cold, or if you've got a period.

Now for some more exercises. Make sure you can do them all, and then see how they fit into your schedule. Remember that young riders must use light weights only – ignore the principle of progression until later.

Press behind neck

Lift to thigh height, pause and then continue to chest height, flicking the weight back on your hands (in other words, just what you *weren't* supposed to do in the high pull). Pause again and then push the bar up carefully and lower it behind your head so that it rests on your shoulders.

If necessary, shuffle your hands and feet a little further apart so that they're comfortable.

Push your arms upwards, breathing in, until they're straight. Pause and lower the bar to your shoulders, breathing out.

The act of lifting from the shoulders and lowering again constitutes one repetition.

Fig. 5 Press behind neck

Standing curl

Lift to thigh height with an underhand grip (with the fingers facing forward). Keep your back straight and your head up, and lift the weight to just below the chin by bending your elbows. Breathe in as you lift. Pause and lower to thigh height again, breathing out as you do so. From thighs to shoulders and back is one repetition.

Fig. 6 Standing curl

Fig. 7 Bent-over rowing

Bent-over rowing

It is absolutely essential to do this exercise correctly, or you'll injure yourself.

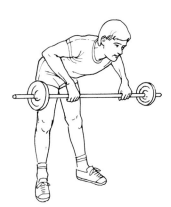

Approach the bar and grasp it overhand. Now make the small of your back as hollow as possible. Stick your bottom out, flex your spine backwards into a kind of banana position and hold it there as stiffly as you can. Lift the bar to chest height, breathing in, and lower to arm's length again, breathing out.

Remember – at no time must you relax your back or use your back muscles for the lift. If you do, serious injury could result. The lift must be entirely by the arms, with the back held rigid.

One bending and straightening of the arms is a repetition.
(NOTE: For safety's sake, it is advisable to do this exercise for the first time under expert supervision.)

Bench press

For this you'll need one of those long, old-fashioned benches or forms (hence the name) that you used at school, and a helper. Lie back along the bench with your head supported and your knees bent over the end of the bench so that your feet are flat on the floor.

Get your helper (or better still, helpers) to hand the bar to you. Grasp it overhand and hold it just clear of your chest, a few inches from the base of your neck. (*Never* hold the bar over your throat or your face, for obvious reasons.)

Push the bar vigorously upwards, breathing out as your arms come straight. Lower the bar carefully and breathe in when your arms are bent again.

The problems of doing this exercise by yourself are fairly clear. What do you do with the bar if things start going wrong, or the weight proves too much? So, don't attempt it unless there's experienced help around to lend a hand.

Fig. 8 Bench press

Leg press

This is a wonderful exercise for bike riders, but you can't do it without special equipment. What you need is a platform which slides up and down on two vertical rods. The principle is that you get under the platform and push it up and down with your feet.

It's no good trying to make one of these legpress machines for yourself unless you just happen to be in that line of business. You can't make them out of old shelves and broom handles, for example, although I've known people try.

If your gym has got one, so much the better. Lie on a mat under the platform, making sure your hips are well the other side of the uprights from your shoulders. Curl up your legs so that your feet are flat on the underside of the board, about shoulder-width apart. Grab hold of the bottom of the uprights for balance's sake and push the platform up and down to your heart's content. (I make that last remark because in at least one gym I've been in, most cyclists have exhausted the stock of weights before they reached their maximum.)

Breathe in as you straighten your legs, and out as you lower the weight.

Oh . . . and do make sure that there are safety stops to prevent the platform coming all the way down. If there aren't, the cleaners may find you still there in the morning, pinned to the ground by the weights.

Oh, oh . . . and do make sure that the weights are properly secured on top of the platform. If they fall off, you won't be in a position to care whether the cleaners find you or not. OK?

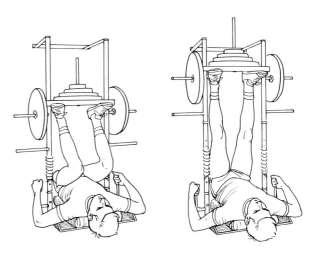

Fig. 9 Leg press

Squat jumps

These are an alternative to leg presses, but not quite as good. They're also not especially good for anyone under 23 because, as I mentioned earlier, you can only take so much weight on an undeveloped spine.

Place the bar across your shoulders in the way you did in the Press behind Neck. Bend your knees carefully until you're halfway between a standing and sitting position. Don't go into a full sitting position, and certainly not into a crouch – just halfway between standing and sitting will do nicely.

Now jump as high as you can, landing gently in an upright position.

You can do the same exercise with dumb-bells in your hands, but it's harder because the limit is the weight your fingers can carry.

A repetition is one jump.

Fig. 10 Squat jumps

Straight arm pull-over

Another exercise you can't perform without a bit of help and supervision.

Get down on the bench as you did for the Bench Press and take the bar in the same way. Straighten your arms as before, but instead of lowering the weight to your chest, keep your arms straight and lower the bar behind you. How low you get with it depends on how flexible your shoulders are and how loose the muscles are in and around your chest. But you should be able to get your arms alongside your ears or maybe even lower. Keep your arms straight. Breathe in as you lower the bar behind you.

Start this exercise with very light weights – if necessary, just with the bar itself – and don't force the movement beyond where it's comfortable. You'll get greater strength and greater range as you improve.

One lower and raise count as a repetition.

Fig. 11 Straight arm pull-over

Power clean

Fig. 12 Power clean

Lift the bar, overhand, to thigh height as you did in the warm-up exercise. Pause, then lift it to chin height (as in the preliminary movement of the Press behind Neck), flipping it back into your hands. Flip it forward again and lower it to the ground in one continuous movement, remembering to bend your knees and not your back.

This is a fast, smooth, almost continuous movement once you've got going and the whole lift and lower counts as one repetition.

Bent arm pull-over

This is exactly the same as the Straight Arm Pull-over, except that you keep your elbows bent. This means that you can pull the weight back with a much more brisk action, so that the bar comes much nearer your face.

Otherwise, the same principles apply as for the Straight Arm Pull-over.

Calf raise

Place the weight on your shoulders as you would for the Press behind Neck. But this time leave it there and just raise slowly on to tip-toe and lower again. One slow raise on to tip-toe and down again is a repetition.

Sit-ups

Sit on the floor with your legs next to each other and straight out in front of you. Hook your feet under something solid (like the wall bars in a gym) and shuffle forward a few inches so that your knees are bent about 90 degrees.

Lie on the floor and clasp your hands behind your neck. Now lift your upper body as far off the floor as you can by twisting upwards. Touch your forehead on your knees.

Fig. 13 Sit-ups

Do this without a weight at first, then start with small weights behind your neck – just the disc itself will do.

A variation is to twist to the side as you sit up, so that you get your right arm to the outside of your left leg on one lift, then your left arm to the outside of your right leg on the next lift, and so on.

There are other variations, still tougher, such as doing the exercise on an inclined board, so that your ankles are higher than your head, but there are slight differences in the effect of the exercise. In every case, though, never do the routine with straight legs – you risk straining your stomach muscles.

There are more weight-training exercises than you'd ever dare imagine, but the foregoing are just some of the most useful for a bikie. The more equipment you've got, the more exotic you can become. If you've got a leg-extension machine, for example, you've got a good way of exercising your thigh muscles without the problems of a leg press.

But what, you say, are the exercises doing? What do I get for the sweat? OK ...

Exercise	*Beneficial to*
Press behind neck	back of upper arms, shoulders, upper back and side of the trunk
Standing curl	hips and back, and especially those muscles which flex the elbow
Bent-over rowing	back muscles
Bench press	chest, front of shoulders, back of upper arms
Leg press	hips, and front and back of upper leg
Squat jumps	thighs, calves, buttocks
Straight arm pull-over	chest expansion, shoulder muscles, front of chest, lower back
Power clean	legs, back, shoulders
Bent arm pull-over	chest and shoulder muscles, lower back, chest expansion
Calf raise	calves, lower back
Sit-ups	front and side stomach muscles

7 Even more about muscles

Each time I've run a weight-training class, I've always wished I could charge a bob a go on the leg-press machine and pay out a pound to anyone doing sit-ups or calf raises. Let's face it, it does seem a lot more relevant, somehow, doing things like leg presses. Give me three sets, I say, and by the time I've unstuck the pea in my whistle I find that they've done about 20.

But the thing about weight training – about *all* training, really – is that it has to be specific to the activity (remember that bit?) but it's also got to be reasonably general. Otherwise you get the strongest legs in the world but your back starts aching after 20 miles. So you have to start with a general routine and then move into the specific.

Here's a beginner's schedule based on one that Eddie Cook worked out and which I've used quite successfully. Remember that the weights are *starting* poundages and that you increase them as I described in the preceding chapter.

Press behind neck	3 sets of 10 reps	25–35 lb
Standing curl	3 sets of 10 reps	25–35 lb
Bent-over rowing	3 sets of 10 reps	35–50 lb
Bench press	3 sets of 8 reps	40–60 lb
Leg press or	3 sets of 6 reps	120–220 lb
Squat jumps	3 sets of 8 reps	25–35 lb
Straight arm pull-over	2 sets of 10 reps	20 lb only
Power cleans	3 sets of 8 reps	35–50 lb

Look at the way Eddie's worked that out and you'll see that it spreads the strain over different groups of muscles. You don't exercise the same groups twice in a row, and yet the work involves the whole body. That's the essence of a good work-out.

Now how about a general routine? This would suit all bikies, but it would particularly suit road racers and general track men.

Power cleans	3 × 10	25 lb
Bench press	3 × 10	35 lb
Standing curl	3 × 10	25 lb
Press behind neck	3 × 10	25 lb
Dorsal hyperextension	3 × 10	No weight
Bent-over rowing	3 × 10	35 lb
Squat jumps	3 × 10	35 lb
Straight arm pull-over	1 × 10	20 lb
Sit-up	3 × 10	No weight
Power cleans	1 × 10	25 lb

The above list includes an exercise which I haven't yet described. A dorsal hyperextension sounds complicated, but it's simple if painful. Lie face down across the edge of a chair or a bench (even a table) and get someone to hold your ankles. Wriggle about until you can lower the upper part of your body over the edge of the bench. Put your hands behind your neck and then lift your body upwards as far as you can, curling your back upwards and craning your head up towards the ceiling. It's a kind of sit-up in reverse.

There are a couple of other points to be made here. The pull-over exercises should always come partway through a schedule because they make you breathe unusually deeply. If you do them without being breathless from other exercises, something called hyperventilation occurs; you take in much more air than your lungs are used to and they become confused and pump a lot of it into your blood. The blood doesn't need it and it dumps a lot of it in your brain, and then that becomes confused, too, and makes you feel dizzy.

It doesn't *always* happen that way, but it might, and feeling dizzy while you're weight training ought to carry a government health warning.

I suppose it's as good a time as any to say that deep breaths at the window first thing in the morning, or before starting a race, are also a bad idea. Same reason – brain gets confused, body goes haywire etc.

The second point is that power cleans turn up twice in the foregoing schedule. That is fairly unusual, but the idea in any good routine is to end up with what's called a 'massive' exercise – one which involves all the main muscle groups. Sit-ups don't do that and there aren't that many exercises that do, hence more power cleans.

Here's Eddie's Cook's routine for time triallists . . .

Power cleans	3 ×	8 reps
Standing curls	3 ×	10 reps
Bent-over rowing	3 ×	6 reps
Bench press	3 ×	8 reps
Leg press	3 ×	8 reps
Straight arm pull-over	2 ×	10 reps

And you could follow that with a few more power cleans, perhaps. Here's one for sprinters . . .

Squat jumps	3 × 10 reps
Single-arm rowing with a dumb-bell	3 × 6 reps
Bent arm pull-over	3 × 8 reps
Leg press	3 × 6 reps
Power cleans	5 × 5, 4, 3, 2, 1 reps, using progressively heavier weights

In the above schedule there's a much greater shift towards strength rather than power, because for a sprinter, especially a track sprinter, acceleration is everything.

The single-arm rowing is just a variation of the ordinary rowing exercise but performed one arm at a time and much more violently. Also the power cleans take on a different character, needing a lot more calculation, as the weights get heavier and the reps fall with each set.

How about hill-climbing?

Upright rowing	3 ×	8 reps
Leg press or squat jump	3 ×	10 reps
Bent arm pull-over	3 ×	8 reps
Calf raise	3 ×	20 reps
Power cleans	3 ×	6 reps

You will no doubt notice that the number of reps – and therefore the potential weight – changes along with the shift from power towards strength. The more strength you need, the more weight you lift and hence the fewer repetitions in each set before you expire.

To achieve the minor variations that you need to make the exercises progressive, try to obtain a set of weights with plenty of small discs. The big ones always seem to be easy to come by because everyone (especially everyone who's given up) goes for the macho image. But it's the $2\frac{1}{2}$ lb and 5 lb discs that are really useful. You won't need anything bigger than 50 lb, perhaps not even bigger than 30 lb, and you won't want more than around 125 lb in total unless you've got access to some of the more fanciful equipment. And do remember, when you calculate your exercises, that the bar itself has a weight – usually 15 lb – so don't leave it out of the total.

Weight-training sessions take between 20 and 40 minutes, depending on how quick you are and the length of your schedule, plus time for setting up and clearing away afterwards. Try always to be methodical. Stack the weights neatly against a wall or you may stagger under a weight, trip and end up under a nurse's critical gaze.

Try to use the weights at least once a week all through the year and maybe as often as three times a week during the winter. Once a week is only four times a month, remember, and if that was road training you wouldn't think much of it, would you?

You'll have to keep riding your bike as well, of course. Remember the old problem of specificity and transfer of fitness. And you can forget all the old tales about muscles turning to fat, or of your body becoming musclebound, or of muscles weighing more than they are worth. Some body-builders build so much bulk around their joints that they can't use them properly. But they do it by using the weights over only a small part of each muscle's range, so that the muscles become bulkier and heavier where they show most. These body-builders don't get much stronger and they get to walk in a funny way, but that's the price of having a body beautiful.

Women can't build massive muscles for the very simple reason that muscle growth depends largely on male hormones. The old claim that cycling gives women big backsides just isn't true. It's mostly fat that's accumulated there *despite* cycling; the problem is that suspending a big, fat bottom on a narrow saddle does rather emphasise the point.

Weight training, even general cycling, will usually enlarge a man's muscles but will simply make a woman's more defined. And muscle won't turn to fat because muscle is muscle and fat is fat. What happens when you stop cycling or weight training is that the muscle wastes away – nature adjusting to demand once again – and the fat that you accumulate through eating the same old amount gets itself all round the muscle fibres so that what was once pure, lean, handsome muscle comes to be an equally large slab of something rather more quivering. Hence female cyclists with big bottoms and thighs. That is an entirely different thing from the muscle becoming fat, and it's entirely within your control to stop it happening.

As your muscles get larger, so your weight will increase for muscle weighs more than fat. But your power will increase too, so that you have surplus power to shift the extra bodyweight and more. Whether you're a skinny type who turns into a good mountain climber, or a big 'un who becomes a track sprinter, depends on where you started off on the somatotype chart on page 27. Mountain climbers are generally less strong than sprinters, but they have less weight to carry and less need for acceleration. Track sprinters can afford to be a bit fat – and often they are – because the extra weight increases their acceleration and the event is too short for it to be a handicap.

8 On the road

All right, down to some more work . . .

Once upon a time, not all that long ago, there was a general theory that cycling taxed the body so much that it was medically essential to do no training at all in the winter. The muscles were tired and full of poisons, the experts said. And the brain would grow stale and weary from being held to a peak for much longer than the racing season.

The odd thing is that training, although a lot more tedious in those days, was actually quite a bit less demanding than now. The main problem with churning out vast numbers of miles is that they're mentally monotonous. The answer used to be to have a break every so often at a café or wherever, and I can still remember the surprise which one of my clubmates expressed in the mid-Sixties when he opened a *Sporting Cyclist* and read that not only did Continental professionals rarely train in shorts, but they didn't stop for a cup of tea either.

Well, it worried us. We wore shorts if it was warm, and we stopped at cafés at the appropriate times, and on reflection the only thing that made our training runs different from a CTC club run is that we called our rides training and they called their rides club runs. Other than that, and about 3 mph, they were much the same. I happily admit that they were very pleasant affairs, and I enjoyed them enormously, but I didn't get very fit and the wildest ambition any of us had was to beat the hour for a '25' (something which, I admit shamefacedly, I have yet to do).

Maybe it was that article we read in the Marshmoor café that night. Or maybe it was the start of a growing realisation that We Were All Doing Something Wrong. But within a couple of years all sorts of things happened and inside three seasons there were mere kids of 14 getting under the hour and thirds and junior road races were becoming hard-scrapped (by the juniors) things and not a kind of high-speed carnival procession.

The one remarkable thing is that some of the old boys back in the Thirties, let alone the Fifties, were doing times which'd be pretty respectable now. You have a look at the records some time, and bear in mind that these Southalls and Frosts and the like were riding tubs like hosepipes on roads that raised dustclouds behind them. And there was no traffic.

Aim for a relaxed, well-balanced position, streamlined but not cramped or extreme. John Herety rides Paris-Nice.

The ideal saddle height means your leg is just a little bent when it's at its straightest. Equally, the perfect frame size brings the top tube between your knees when the cranks are horizontal – as Sid Barras shows.

Boy, if only they knew then what we know now.

Well, enough of this. The point is that higher demands mean higher investments, and training is an all-round-the-year business. You can see that from this circle of training.

We've done the circuit and weight training. How about the road?

Remember that if you've been riding all year to get some effect from the gym training, there'll be no real rough to ride off in the weeks after Christmas. Just when you start proper road training depends on when you want to start racing, when you want to reach your peak, and on the weather.

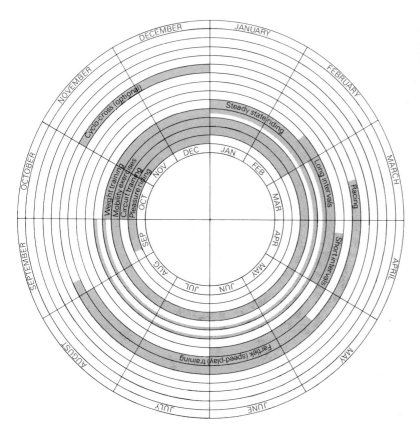

Fig. 14 Typical circle of training for a senior roadman

The season has been starting earlier and finishing sooner during recent years, but the weather hasn't taken much notice. You think back on how many times the weeks from Christmas to the middle of January have been fine and everyone's been out training with the joy of an early spring inside them. And then, bang on cue, February's brought the sleet and the snow and everything you built up has gone to pot.

It's not for nothing that the richer professional teams all shoot off to the south of France and to Italy for the first weeks of the year. It may not be exactly sunbathing weather there, but it beats Wakefield.

Rule one: don't let over-enthusiasm force you into anything you might regret.

Something else you may like to think about: there is no point in training for any great distance if you race for 50 miles or less. And if your racing is right down to ten miles, or just a few kilometres on the track, is there much point in distance training at all?

Rule two: don't train the way everyone else does for no other reason than that.

And . . .

Rule three: don't think that if training is good for you then lots and lots of it must be even better.

In 1976, Ed Burke looked at what had happened to racing cyclists after their off-season. What he and his colleagues found was that there was no great fall-off in aerobic ability (riding at less than oxygen debt, you remember) but that anaerobic ability (going absolutely flat out for short but vital bursts) had taken a nose-dive.

In other words, assuming that you've had an active winter, with a bit of cycling, or skating, or backpacking and so on, and some gym training, you'll probably have kept most of your stamina but not your speed. Your strength, or power, may well have increased because of your weight training.

In the shadow of the stars: riding on a wheel – as close as possible to the rider in front – saves a massive amount of energy. Francesco Moser puts on the pressure during a world championship, and the world's best follow.

Why, then, go in for massive miles in your early-season training when the evidence shows that's exactly what you're least likely to need? Oh sure, if you're new to the sport, or you've had a long lay-off, or there are similar circumstances, it may be different. But if you raced last year and you kept active most of the winter, this is all about you.

The chances are that, unless you're riding road races of 80 miles or more, or long-distance time trials, you could start training much later than the post-Christmas early-birds, forgo some of the long rides and get started on something more valuable – like speed work, because speed wins races.

You can work out your start-off policy for yourself by thinking about what it is you'll be riding for most of the season. According to Ed Burke, applying observation to established figures, it looks like this . . .

Event	Time of race	Flat-out	Speed	Cruising
100 m road race	3h55 – 4h	0%	5%	95%
100 km criterium	2:05 – 2:15	5%	10%	85%
100 km team TT	2:10 – 2:20	0%	15%	85%
25 m time trial	:52 – 1:00	0%	10%	90%
25 m criterium	:50 – 1:00	5%	15%	80%
10 m track	20 min – 25 min	10%	20%	70%
4 km ind pursuit	4:45 – 5:05	20%	55%	25%
Kilometre	1:07 – 1:13	80%	15%	5%
Match sprints	:11 – :13	98%	2%	0%

Here, 'flat-out' means using entirely alternative energy, quite independent of breathing; 'speed' means fast enough to reach the limit of the usefulness of breathing, plus partial use of lactic acid (the stuff which produces oxygen debt and aching muscles); and 'cruising' means within the limits of the oxygen sent to the muscles, although on the road this can still be pretty fast.

'Some of the percentages in the longer events may seem out of proportion,' says Ed Burke, 'but think about the event for a moment. In a 100-mile road race lasting 250 minutes (4h10), five per cent would be 12.5 minutes. This is a long time to be using anaerobic sources.'

Now that you can see just what your event demands, you can see the kind of training that needs to go into it, especially if you look at the next table. This one shows the degree to which different training methods (which I'll explain) produce different effects. Again, I'm grateful to Ed Burke for putting it into figures.

Type of training	Speed	Stamina
Steady slow riding	5%	95%
Steady fast riding	15%	85%
Repetition riding	60%	40%
Fartlek	50%	50%
Intervals	50%	50%
Set sprints	80%	20%
Acceleration sprints	90%	10%
Sprint training	95%	5%

Don't let that word 'steady' catch you out, nor the word 'slow'. This is about racing and not wafting round the Cotswolds with a saddlebag. 'Steady' simply means that there are no sudden accelerations; 'slow' merely means less than full race speed. By these standards, you can be going 'slow' and still have a heart rate of around 150 beats a minute.

You should try that one day; ride five miles or so at the speed you'd ride a '25', then sit up and take your heart rate by feeling the carotid artery at the side of your throat, below the jawbone. It won't be much different from 150 – it might be even less – so you can see that the kind of training that you see most people doing round the dual carriageways of Britain ranks as 'slow' in this context.

'Steady slow riding' means longer than the race distance. To a sprinter, that could be 25 miles. To a roadman, that may mean 125 miles in one session.

'Steady fast riding' is still longer than race distance but not quite as long as slow riding. A junior riding 50-mile road races may train over 65 miles, for example, or a 3 km pursuiter over 4,000 metres.

Because the heart remains at a steady pace, this kind of training's called 'steady state'. The problem with the name is that it gives the wrong idea.

'Too many people concentrate on the steady rather than getting into a state,' is how junior coach Les Jordan put it.

This kind of riding opens the blood capillaries in the muscles and re-teaches the skill of smooth pedalling. It's more important to riders who've had a longish lay-off, or who haven't remained active during the winter. It was always called Getting The Rough Off in years gone by, and if your body's overweight and creaking a bit then I suppose it's no bad description. The Belgian doctor, Gerard Daniëls, reckons that suppleness and general pedalling skill and efficiency stem from training at first on low gears turned quickly. I'm pretty sure most of the world's coaches would agree with that.

To Daniëls, that initial training should be with a gear no higher than around five-sixths of the maximum allowed in the appropriate category – around 72 for juniors for example, or, say, 86 for seniors. That would provide endurance – local muscular endurance – and he'd go still lower if he was looking more for pedalling skill.

I don't regard this pedalling skill as being as unimportant as it may at first sound ('Anybody here forgotten how to pedal?' etc). And for the same reason I've never been sure why riders who intend to race on gears spend some of their winter training on fixed. If we get back to the principle of specificity, the argument of mechanical simplicity is overcome by the fact that you're training for something quite different. I suppose if you're going to ride on fixed then it's an entirely different matter, but hardly anybody rides fixed in time trials these days, in road races you're not allowed to, and track specialists would not be venturing out on the road for any great distance in winter anyway.

If you haven't kept up your training all winter, ride for about a quarter longer than your mid-season race distance (unless you're riding '12s' or '24s', of course). Otherwise, start training once you know the weather's going to stay at least tolerable and stick to a maximum of three-quarters of your maximum race distance. That means juniors would train up to about 40 miles, seniors to around 75, in one session. And even that would need to be built up to, because the emphasis still has to be on riding the distance as fast as you can – 'slow' in training terms, but still at your best time trial speed.

Try to do it at least three evenings a week and once at weekends, although be flexible; it's better to stay indoors than risk your neck in fog or ice. Schoolboys and trackies can start later and with fewer, shorter sessions. Just look at that second table again and you'll get an idea of what you need.

After a few rides, split your training rides into quarters. Decide before you set out where you are going and set the quarter-distances that way. Pedal as fast as you can manage, without sprinting, over the first quarter. Then ride gently but still quickly until you're recovered, before tackling the second quarter and repeating until you've done all four with the full distance covered.

Remember that even 'slow' training turns out – or should turn out! – to be pretty fast by winter standards.

I've always believed that most riders need far fewer 'basic' winter miles than they pile in. Road racing is certainly an endurance sport – 95 per cent of it over 100 miles – but the endurance/stamina aspect falls as the distance decreases, and there aren't a great many riders who specialise in road races of 100 miles or more.

If you look at a marathon runner – and two hours of running link quite closely with four hours of cycling – you'll find that the training period is by no means as long, or the training itself so time consuming. This, I believe, says a lot. It says, especially, that athletics training is more advanced than cycling's (greater performance from less training time) and it says, too, that runners are generally less obsessed with sheer mileage as a recipe for success.

Once you can cover your race distance at however slow a speed, your only interest is in covering it faster. You won't get appreciably faster by covering the same distance time after time, so the only gains must be psychological ('I know I've done 100 miles in training, so I won't get shot off . . .') and technical ('I've done 100 miles in training, so I know I won't get saddle sore, I know how much food to eat, how much water to drink, how to pedal efficiently . . .').

I would guess that most juniors who have prepared during the winter, and who have raced before, would need around 500 miles of steady-state training before going further, and some seniors would need around 1,000 miles. When Norman Sheil was national coach, he told riders aspiring to the Olympic Squad that they should have covered 2,000 miles by the end of February, but this was to riders already extensively coached in training methods and meant 'quality' training rather than simple miles.

By the time the basic 500 or 1,000 miles of steady fast riding are out of the way, start thinking more about speed. I said before – once you can cover the race distance at any speed, you're interested only in doing it faster. And you'll only do it faster by splitting the total into shorter intermediate stretches. You ride the shorter stretches as fast as you can, have a breather, and then do it again. I call this long-interval training; Ed Burke calls it repetition riding.

The idea is to take yourself to the edge of oxygen debt – to ride so that you're using all the oxygen you can get into your blood, without calling on the reserve lactic acid system – and then slowing enough for your body to recover. It would take a laboratory to work out just how long each session needs to be, but who's got a spare boffin standing by? You'll have to do what the rest of us do, and guess.

Start by riding for 15 minutes at the speed you'd do in a 10-mile time trial. Keep the speed up all the time, but keep the gears lower than you'd use in a race and don't get out of the saddle and sprint at any time. When the 15 minutes are up, change down gear, sit up and pootle along at about 12 miles an hour. Don't stop or freewheel – you'll recover better if you keep pedalling lightly.

A 200-metre sprint is the most you can manage at top speed because your body switches over to alternative energy that lasts only that long. Sean Kelly shows the benefits of oxygen debt and muscular power on the track at Roubaix.

Ride steadily for about seven minutes, then wind up into your time trial speed for another 15 minutes. Don't sprint away when you start the hard bash. The idea is to come as close to oxygen debt as you can without actually going into it. Keep the routine going until you've been out on the road for about three-quarters of your race time. In other words, train for about three hours if you're riding 100-mile time trials or road races, or for about an hour and a half if you're interested in '50s'.

Taking yourself to the edge of oxygen debt brings us back to the principle of overloading and overadjustment. Remember them? Ride to that limit and you're actually pushing that limit further back and increasing your resistance. You improve your cruising rate (have a look at that chart again), and the better your cruising rate the firmer the base for pure speed training later on.

It's at this stage that (I promise you) something wonderful will happen. After a short while, you'll find that you don't need seven minutes to recover from 15 minutes of hard hammering. You'll only need five minutes. My goodness, you say to yourself, what progress I'm making. I wish I'd actually bought the book instead of getting it out of the library.

But don't get complacent. The routine now is to shorten the rest periods little by little until you've recovered almost completely after just two minutes. When this happens, you'll know that your lungs and arteries and veins and all the other stuff inside you have been taught a pretty good lesson; when you want the old muck cleared out of your muscles sharpish, you'll have it cleared out sharpish and there'll be no argument.

When you get down to two minutes' rest time, *shorten* the fast period to ten minutes instead of 15. Don't make it longer – that would only make you go more slowly. Shorten it to ten minutes and this time ride like you'd ride if a million dollars depended on it. No sprinting, no big gears, no getting out of the saddle; just solid, sustained flat-out riding, like a world championship pursuit.

See how long it takes you to recover from that. You might be back to the ten minutes again, but it doesn't matter. Repeat as before, keeping the fast time the same but reducing the recovery period as you get fitter until you find you only need a couple of minutes. Then shorten the fast periods even more, until you're riding flat out for just a mile and a half, maybe two miles.

But remember – flat out means as fast as you possibly can without getting out of the saddle or using big gears; recovery means, in this case, your breathing getting back to normal. It's a lung exercise, so don't go belting off again until your breathing's settled right down.

And if you thought this was hard, just you wait and see what comes next.

9 Icicles and bicycles

But first, a word of warning. Riding about like a bat out of hell does all sorts of things to your body temperature. Any doctor who looked at an athlete in training, without realising it, would have no hesitation in giving him time off work. He might even send him to hospital. Your temperature goes up to fever pitch, your blood pressure zooms all over the place, your blood sugar drops, your eyes go all red and sometimes you feel every bit as sick as the doctor thinks you ought to feel.

Oh, it's not dangerous. Not if you're normally healthy and you haven't got a duff heart or you've spent the last decade drinking Guinness and watching horse racing. No, the point is this: here you are, apparently dying with something like eight chapters of a medical textbook on odd diseases, and you're out on cold winter evenings making a fool of yourself.

If you go out when the temperature's at freezing point and you ride at 20 mph into a 15 mph wind – a pretty gentle wind – you've actually created a private Arctic gale around yourself. It's called wind chill, and it means that the faster the air moves around you, the colder it will feel. It may be just freezing for someone standing still, but for you on the move it's minus 10 Centigrade.

It depends where you live, but wind chill can be merely inconvenient, or it can set your training back quite handsomely, or you could get frostbite or worse. Have a look at the chart overleaf.

There's no point in getting over-alarmed. But it is worth knowing what the risks are, especially if you live somewhere cold or flat and exposed.

You can judge the wind fairly easily. At 20 mph, small branches move on trees and dust and snow blow up; at 30 mph you can see large branches moving; and at 40 mph, whole trees move. A wind that you can just feel on your face will be about 10 mph.

Wind+riding mph	Air temperature (F)							
	50	40	30	20	10	0	−10	−20
5	48	37	27	16	6	−5	−15	−26
10	40	28	16	4	−9	−24	−33	−46
15	36	22	9	−5	−18	−32	−45	−58
20	32	18	4	−10	−25	−39	−53	−67
25	30	16	0	−15	−29	−44	−59	−74
30	28	13	−2	−18	−33	−48	−63	−79
35	27	11	−4	−20	−35	−51	−67	−82
40	26	10	−6	−21	−37	−53	−69	−85
	LITTLE DANGER				RISING DANGER			GREAT DANGER

The wind has less effect when it comes from the back or the side, so you could plan your training route accordingly. Go out into the wind and come back with it when you're feeling more tired and sweatier. Or better still, organise your training into a fairly local circuit that you cover several times. The benefit of this is that you're never far from home if things go a bit wrong.

Muscles work much less efficiently in the cold, and you can protect them by wearing several thin layers. Modern cycle-training clothing is good, but you'll need several layers underneath – long underpants, racing shorts and several vests or thin jumpers, with a heavier layer on top.

Avoid elasticated fittings if you can, because they become sweat bands of potentially freezing water. Use braces. And do try one of those more recent inventions, the vest that wicks sweat away from the body and into a T-shirt. They cost a bit more than usual, but they're worth the price. Don't ask me how they do it, but they absorb sweat from the body and, instead of holding it like a normal cotton or woollen vest, they pass it on to the next layer. You stay dry but the second layer gets damp.

Never ride without a hat in the winter. You lose a lot of your body heat through your head. And you can keep your feet warm by wearing specially-made overshoes or simply by wearing two pairs of socks with a plastic bag in between the pairs. And remember that mittens are warmer than gloves, and that gloves worn inside mittens are the warmest of all.

I remember being in Belgium, riding from Zeebrugge to Bruges and being grateful that my hat folded down into a balaclava. Frostbite is not something unique to polar explorers. It, and its cousin – wind nip, can happen to bikies as well and can have serious effects. The temperature doesn't have to drop far below freezing for hands, ears, noses, toeses and the rest to get painful and then start losing sensation. If this happens, stop! Don't rub the frozen parts or try to walk on frozen feet. Place frozen fingers under your armpits or in your groin. As soon as you can, put the affected parts in water heated to body temperature and call a doctor. It's no joke – it's very serious.

All right . . . on with the action . . .

IO You're all heart...

By the time you can keep thrashing away for three hours — even two hours — at a mile and a half at a time, you're going to be pretty fit by anybody's standards. But *pretty* fit is what the next guy is. It's not good enough.

The problem is that the training which'll really make you fast is also pretty mind-stunningly dull. It works, by golly it works. But there's no point in doing it all the time because within a fortnight you'll have taken up darts or gardening or going out with women.

You see, if we get back to basics, the winner in any race is the man who went fastest, even if it was only for a tiny part of the race. He went faster than you out of a corner, or over a hill, or away from the start, or in the final sprint. It doesn't matter where; the point is that somewhere, for just a moment, he went faster than you did. So unless *you're* the fastest in the race, you'll win only by luck or by surprise.

If the fastest you can ride is sprinting speed, and the furthest you can sprint is about 200 yards, then you can see the problem. You have to sprint that kind of distance repeatedly.

The training covered so far has concentrated on getting oxygen into the blood, the blood to the muscles, the wastes back out of the muscles, and so on. Your lungs work better, your blood flows more easily and, in the process, your heart has grown larger. That is, instead of being like a paper bag that holds four ounces of bullseyes, it's now like one of those plastic bags that you use to bring potatoes back from the supermarket.

Each time your heart beats, therefore, it pushes out more blood than it did previously. Your body also needs less blood than it did, so you'll probably have noticed that your heart rate has fallen.

To get a very simplified image of your heart, cup your hands together as if they were holding an orange. The orange represents the blood. The bigger the orange, the bigger cup your hands make. Close your hands suddenly and there's no room for the orange. That's what happens to the blood in your heart, and it squirts out into the arteries.

But unless you make your hands stronger, you can't close them any faster than you do at the moment. The more room you have to leave for the orange, the longer it takes you. Likewise with your heart – the more it swells, the more blood it contains but the longer it takes to empty itself.

The more long-interval or steady-state training you do, the larger your heart becomes and the more blood it contains. The muscle surrounding the heart will grow stronger as well, but not at the same rate. That's the mark of an endurance athlete.

Among sportsmen with the largest hearts, therefore, you'd expect to find long-distance cyclists (in this case Tour de France riders), followed by marathon runners, other long-distance runners, rowers and boxers.

The significant thing is that sprinters – specialist cycling sprinters, that is – have hearts larger than middle-distance runners and weight-lifters – but still very much smaller than Tour de France riders. Here's the reason . . .

The more violent the acceleration required, the more the muscles require blood in a very great hurry. They can survive oxygen debt for a short while, but the lactic-acid system is like money in your pocket – you can spend it freely while it lasts but it needs replacing immediately afterwards.

The amount of blood needed isn't necessarily all that much – hence the smaller heart volume – but the speed of delivery is all important. And it can only be delivered in a hurry if the heart muscle is very strong, if it can make the heart contract powerfully and suddenly.

As a general rule, the heart starts getting larger when working at around 90 beats a minute. The exact figure isn't important, but even moderate exercise will do it. By 120 beats a minute the heart muscle's shifting enough weight – blood – for it to be doing its own weight training, so it gets more powerful. From 140 beats on, the effect is remarkable. It doesn't even matter whether you're riding or resting at the time; provided it's hammering away at 120 or more, the muscle's getting stronger.

Like a lot else about our athletic performance, the way the heart works is largely pre-determined. Sprinters are probably born with smaller and stronger hearts than people who turn into champion time triallists. It's all a matter of what you're 'good at' in the first place. But you can go too far.

It's possible, by constantly riding long distances at less than 120 beats a minute, to develop a heart so large but so floppy that it will never respond properly to sudden demands. The muscle is just too weak to oblige at high speeds, although it's perfect for cruising in time trials at 25 mph.

And it's possible, too, to take an already small heart and thicken and strengthen the heart muscle so much that the fabric is too taut to stretch. The heart then becomes good for sports which need sudden short bursts of acceleration. Dr Peter Travers, who works at Exeter University, believes that this is a very good reason why schoolboys should not do interval training (which thickens the heart) and also why many schools ought to change their physical exercise policy. More stamina, less speed is his demand for youngsters. Once your heart is fully grown or enlarged, he argues, that's the time to start developing it further.

The middle route on the diagram is what he'd aim for.

Fig. 15 How your heart responds to training

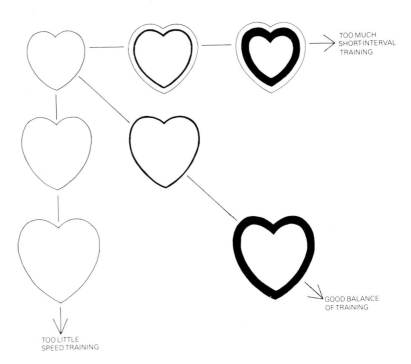

TOO MUCH SHORT-INTERVAL TRAINING

GOOD BALANCE OF TRAINING

TOO LITTLE SPEED TRAINING

It is possible to get the heart up to about 220 beats a minute, but by then even the best heart will be unable to contract and open fully in the time. When you hear people say that something set their heart 'all of a flutter', that's just what they mean.

So how *do* you get your heart rate high enough . . .

First you need a gear big enough to sprint in. Not enormous, because you need good acceleration as well, but big enough. Then sprint for 200 yards, entirely flat out, legs, knees and arms going everywhere, absolutely no attention to style. Just all-out effort for 200 yards.

Brake hard and find the artery on the side of your neck, just below the jaw bone. (You'll have to be quick because even now your heart rate will already be falling.) Count how many times your heart beats in six seconds (you'll need a watch with a second hand, or a posh digital one). Time how long it takes before the beats fall to 12 in six seconds, then sprint off again immediately.

By this stage you'll still be breathing hard. You certainly won't feel rested in the way you did with the long-interval training. But what you've got to do is complete the second sprint, pause for the same number of seconds as you did after the first sprint (no need to time the heartbeats again), then sprint again, have another rest, sprint for a fourth time, and then feel thoroughly ill.

By the time you've finished four sprints, you'll feel so shattered that I doubt you'll be able to manage a fifth one at anything like the right speed, so go for a gentle ride on low gears until your breathing's back to normal again — just as it would have been during the long-interval training. Then complete another set of four sprints, have a second rest, and carry on like this until in total you've done 16 or, better still, 20 sprints.

In all that time, if the rest periods between individual sprints are short enough, your heart will have been thrashing away all the time at between 120 and 180 or more beats a minute, getting stronger all the time. The longer rest periods between every set of four sprints are to let the rest of your body recover, because a healthy heart can take any amount of this treatment.

Carry out a test sprint at the start of each day's session because your recovery period (down to 12 beats every six seconds) will get slightly shorter each time until in the end it just bottoms out. Don't make the gap between each sprint even a couple of seconds longer than it has to be, don't lengthen or shorten the sprinting distance, and don't be tempted to ease up a little before the 200 yards are covered.

Now, fair warning . . . effective though this kind of training is, it's pretty dull. In fact, all *real* training is less interesting than going out in a chain gang with the lads. But there's no reason why you shouldn't mix it. (More about that in the section on training schedules later on.) For the moment though, just think about short-interval sprinting before going for a longer steady-state ride (you won't feel like it, but you'll be quite capable once your body's calmed down a bit), and about variations in interval sprinting.

You could try kermesse sprinting. For this, you need a flat square of roads with sides of around 400 yards. Factory estates are often good sites because they're quiet in the evening and at weekends. The car park of the local Tesco mega-store on a Saturday morning is never as convenient.

Use the same routine as for the pure sprints, but don't worry about heart rates. Have a gentle ride round the circuit a couple of times, then sprint along 200 yards of one straight, absolutely flat out. Brake hard 100 yards before the corner, freewheel round it and for another 100 yards, then sprint to 100 yards short of the next corner, and so on. Keep going like that for a full circuit.

Remember, it has to be a 100 per cent sprint and it has to be 200 yards. The gaps round the corners are your recovery periods. And remember, too – just four sprints before taking a rest.

Kermesse sprinting is less precise than pure interval sprinting because you're not timing your rests or taking your heart rate. But then they're difficult things to do on a bike in the first place. So long as the effort is brief and intense, and the recovery periods are no more than you need to be able to sprint again, the same benefits should be there. If you've followed the routine through, the gap between sets of four sprints should be down to just a couple of minutes.

Aim for 16 or 20 sprints, building to around 40 when you get really good at it.

I don't usually advise sprinting against a buddy simply because the winner of each sprint tends to ease off just before the imaginary line, or the loser starts giving up a bit, and everything begins to go haywire. There's no reason why the two of you shouldn't use the same circuit at the same time, though, maybe even in different directions, because at least then you'll have a bit of companionship and someone to ride home with afterwards.

There are other variations, too. Try pulse pedalling. On the way back from work or school, ride a couple of miles and then start sprinting for 200 yards and resting for 150. Or you could try sprinting between two (or three) lamp-posts at a time. Anything, really, that sustains the interval effect and keeps your heart beating really fast.

Or you could try ladder sprinting, which gives you intervals of all sorts of length. You need a long, straight and reasonably wide road. I once lived near the driveway of a large, stately home and since his lordship didn't realise I was bringing a bunch of scruffy bike riders to use his grounds twice a week, I don't suppose he had cause to object. Anyway, I was grateful to his ancestors for building such admirable private roads.

Mark the road off in 100-yard intervals, or lamp-post stretches. Sprint 100 yards, turn round and ride briskly but not fast back to the start. Turn round and sprint to the 200-yard point. Carry on riding back to the start and extending the sprinting distance by 100 yards until you're sprinting around 500 yards. Then rest a bit and go again.

Once you're sprinting much past 200 yards at a time, your heart rate either won't go up as high or it'll go up and start coming back down again even while you're riding. This means that ladder sprinting isn't as efficient as the other variations, but it can be more entertaining.

His lordship's grounds used to provide moments of comic relief, too. I never objected to groups carrying out ladder sprinting as a race provided the road was wide enough for everyone to turn in safety and not cause impressive pile-ups or burning brake blocks.

The trouble is that once you get a race going, nobody wants to ease up on the way back to the start. And if you don't ease up, the whole thing degenerates into a dotty time trial and nobody benefits.

We couldn't see any way round the problem until, for a laugh, someone suggested riding back to the start on one leg. It sounds absolutely ludicrous but it both worked and caused so many laughs that we experimented with riding back with one hand and even with looking sideways (this in a moment of hysteria and giggling and on a private road, remember, and miraculously with nobody ever falling off). It was crazy but it worked and it turned out to be fun as well, which is just what cycling should be, however seriously you take it.

Many riders think heart rates are a lot of old rubbish. They accuse coaches of taking all the fun out of the sport by concentrating more on their stopwatches than on the real game. I think they're probably right to scoff. You can go overboard about it all. You can make it terribly dull and earnest. But you can also learn a lot about yourself by simply checking your heart rate every so often, especially during exercise. If you don't know what your heart is doing, and what is happening to you when it's doing it, you're in a pretty poor position to know how to train and whether your training is doing you any good.

Interval training isn't the be-all of bike racing. Not all bike racing, anyway. Its importance increases as the demand for sheer speed rises, and you can see that from the diagram on page 69.

Before we leave the subject for a while, let me just tell you something very odd about heart rates and recovery times. When you have ridden steady state, in other words so that you breathe in all the oxygen that your body needs, your pulse rate will start falling as soon as you stop the exercise. But if you go into oxygen debt, just the opposite applies. Instead of falling, it will carry on rising for several seconds. And when it starts falling again, it falls irregularly. On a graph, it would look like this:

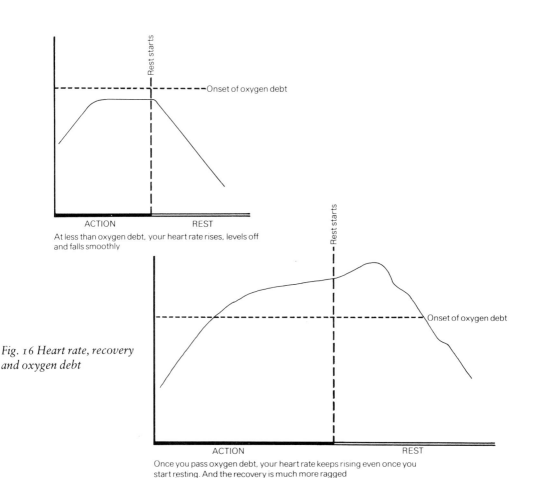

Fig. 16 Heart rate, recovery and oxygen debt

At less than oxygen debt, your heart rate rises, levels off and falls smoothly

Once you pass oxygen debt, your heart rate keeps rising even once you start resting. And the recovery is much more ragged

You can translate this into bike racing quite easily. The top graph shows what happens for most of the time in a road race and for all the time in a time trial, if it's ridden properly. Your heart rate will rise until it reaches the point at which it's carrying all the oxygen and sugars that the muscles need.

In a time trial, or a track pursuit, the ideal would be to get your heart rate as near to the oxygen debt line as you can and hold it there, turning out constantly maximum cruising speed.

The only exception would be the start period in which the effort of leaving the timekeeper, especially in a pursuit, would push the body into oxygen debt.

In a road race, the line would wobble somewhat more as the demands of the moving bunch rose and fell. But whenever someone attacked and you sprinted, or you hammered up a hill or out of a corner, you would go into oxygen debt and your heart rate would rise above the oxygen debt line. The same would happen through inconsistent riding in a pursuit or a time trial.

You can sustain partial oxygen debt for some time, but you can only cope with *total* oxygen debt for about 15 seconds. Then you have to ease right up – you don't have a choice. In a pursuit or time trial it's called 'blowing up'. It means losing a pursuit because the distance available for recovery is so short. The effects in a time trial are both physical and mental, because bad oxygen debt breaks morale, shatters riding rhythm and ruins your concentration.

In a road race it's your most vulnerable period. Because you know what happens to you when you attack on the flat, or up a hill, you gamble that it'll happen, only more so, to everyone else. And, if your training has been correct and you're not competing against riders of a much higher quality, that will be so. An effective move is to rise cautiously to someone else's hard attack on a hill, wait until it's been going about 20 seconds and then attack for yourself. In this way you exploit the other rider's oxygen debt.

But what if he does it to you? Well, you have to rely on the efficiency of your metabolism not taking you too far through the danger line.

Now, maybe, you see why heart rates are so important.

11 Skill is all

There've been coaches in the past who've sworn that group training –
bit-and-bit, chain gangs and so on – are absolutely worthless. I've
been at coaching seminars and heard them rant on about their evils,
about how everybody comes down to the level of the weakest rider
who manages to hang on to the group, how the best riders can't ride to
their potential, how everybody has to settle for an average. And it's all
quite true. They're correct. But I still don't agree with them.

I don't agree because training entirely by yourself, all the time, is a
very odd form of preparation for a sport in which you ride against
other people.

Group training will never be as fast as short intervals, but it does
other important things, even for riders like pursuiters and match
sprinters who ride in very small groups. And even – or especially – for
time triallists, who race entirely alone. It teaches goodwill, humour
and companionship, which are what keep you in the sport. It teaches
tactics, anticipation and observation. And it teaches bike control
which, when you see the way some very prominent time triallists go
round roundabouts as if they had pitted headsets, is very important. It
also gives you a pretty good guide to how fit you're getting.

Where some groups go wrong, though, is that they're too large and
that they ride too far from home. Six is a good number for a
chain-gang group, riding a circuit of about five miles rather than an
out-and-home route. Six riders means there's not a lot of chance that
they'll have hugely differing abilities. And a five-mile circuit means a
rider who's been dropped or had a puncture can ride back in the other
direction and join in again as the group passes. Surely nothing's so
dispiriting and counter-productive than to be left shattered and
exhausted with 30 miles to ride in a headwind?

It's also a matter of skill, and unless you ride in a group you're neglecting, even for a time triallist, one of the component parts of fitness. I do hate to go on about the early-one-morning brigade, but if ever you wanted to see the most awkward ways to take corners, the most curious riding styles and the most odd ways of doing almost anything, the place to be just has to be a time trial. The other extreme, the joy of watching beautiful bike handling, anticipation and sheer general skill is to watch the polished perfection of a good cyclo-cross rider.

Fast cornering means putting all your weight on your outside leg and arm. Indeed, Bernard Hinault has shifted so much weight outwards that he can take his right hand off the bars to change gear.

Racing abroad brings techniques of its own. In Belgium, for example, the road's often bad and riders switch to the cyclepath. Then, when the road gets better again, you get some on one side, some on the other. Hennie Kuiper leads Sean Yates.

And if you think you're pretty good already, just listen to a tale that a friend told me by way of evidence. He was a former semi-professional – an independent they called them in those days – who after many years of racing here went to try his hand in Belgium.

In those days, Belgian courses were very small and had riders by the hundred. He'd always reckoned his bike handling was above average and the conditions didn't worry him. He didn't understand a word of what anybody was saying, and if they turned out to be swearing, well, so what?

It turned out they were swearing about him, though, and eventually someone did something about it. He was taking a left-hander when an arm reached across to his handlebars. A hand grabbed the bars and started turning them for him. He never saw the body on the other end; he was too terrified to look. He got round the corner without harm, but it persuaded him that even his best wasn't good enough.

It's quite a feat to steer your own bike on cobbles at that speed; to control someone else's as well is out of this world!

The skill of time trialling, of course, is not so apparent. But skill there is, nevertheless – right at the start we saw it was the ability to pace your effort right through the distance. Too far from the anaerobic (oxygen debt) line and you finish with energy to spare. Too frequently over it and you have to spend part of the race recovering or, worse still, you end with a sugar deficiency (which I'll get to later).

Team time trials demand specialised skill and a high cruising rate. Most are for teams of two, three or four; in the Tour de France, ten may ride at a time.

It stands to reason, too, that the type of mental concentration needed in a time trial is different from that of a road-race rider. I doubt it's any more or less; it's just different. The circumstances of a time trial are under your own control, so you pitch yourself against them – the weather, the road surface, the distance and so on – at your own level. The mental effort, therefore, is more one of complete detach-ment from anything not concerned with turning out the highest cruising rate, whereas roadmen have both the circumstances and the other riders to cope with. In a time trial, the effort has to be spread evenly over the whole distance, whereas at times the roadman has to gamble more of his effort than he'd choose, to exploit a rival's weakness or to compensate for his own.

Achieving that ability is what makes many time triallists go faster as the season progresses. Unless there's specific speed training, the only increase in cruising rate comes from better weather, better pace judging, and the incidental but not primary benefits of steady-state training. The training that most time triallists seem to do – plugging away alone on gears close to those they use in races – merely makes their bodies better at riding 50 or 100 miles or whatever. They can cover the distance more comfortably but it's debatable whether they can cover it very much faster.

The whole nature of time trialling has changed in the last 20 or 30 years, too. Riders have swung almost entirely from fixed wheel to gears, and at the same time the gears have risen vastly. When Norman Sheil broke the British '25' record, it was on a fixed wheel of around 86 inches. There are riders now using gears half as big again, but the improvement in times have been much less. In fact if riders who shove vast gears tried to do so on the roads (and with the same kind of passing traffic) that Sheil and the rest used, I doubt there'd be any real difference in time.

Most of the records that have fallen in the last 15 years appear to have toppled because of the quantity of passing traffic causing a 'push and suck' effect. This is one aspect that never occurs to Americans and Continentals when they see how easily they can beat us at almost everything except, in theory, time trialling. It's only at time trialling that we rarely meet on our own ground, and when we have – such as when the RTTC ran international events near Reading – the Continentals may not have won but they came staggeringly close to our best, despite the tremendous difference in acquired skill.

For this reason, there are no small number of people who believe that time-trial records – or, at least, the times set on 'normal' courses without heavy traffic – should be historically higher than they are. The argument is that riders don't foster the simple skills they'd get from chain-gang riding and cyclo-cross; their training isn't intensive enough; and they ride gears that are too high for them.

This, from time to time, is one of the biggest arguments that time-trialling produces. The big gears versus the moderate gears.

Official feeling – the national coaching scheme and the rules of the RTTC in some junior and schoolboy events – is that big gears for young riders are bad. So far as I know, there is no evidence either way. In fact, tests in America showed that well-trained young riders were at no physiological disadvantage when it came to riding against seniors on senior terms.

Vaughan Thomas, the boffin who thought we ought to be doing more weight training, said:

> Because pedalling machines were easiest to set up in laboratories, cycling became the main subject of these (cadence) investigations, and a whole stream of suggestions came forth over the years, that cyclists would perform more efficiently when pedalling at rates anywhere between 30 and 60 per minute.

Cadence is the rate of repeating an activity such as pedalling, and 30 to 60 a minute is fairly slow by normal standards. Dr Thomas went on: 'However, racing cyclists have never been ones to swallow everything boffins tell them, and they went on their way pedalling at between 90 and 120 revolutions a minute.'

Then he gave the cadence figures for different sportsmen:

Oarsmen	35–40
Swimmers (arms)	40–50
Canoeists	40–50
Walkers	75–85
Runners	55–65
Cyclists	90–120

Walkers, of course, have an unusually high rate because their rules oblige them to keep in contact with the ground all the time, which means an abnormally short stride. Dr Thomas draws from the figures and his own investigations that racing cyclists simply pedal too rapidly.

'My own feeling,' he said, 'is that cyclists tend to be under-geared, to use too high a cadence rate than is *physiologically* sound.' The italics are his, not mine.

Now, it's obvious that lower gears produce better acceleration and that you need a few inches in hand in a road race if someone is going to launch an attack any moment. But too low a gear can be tiring and tired legs tend to go not, as you might think, for a lower gear but for a higher one. You've only got to follow a Continental classic to see that – the way very experienced roadmen go up a gear in the last 30 or 40 miles with no apparent change of pace and at just the time when they might most expect the important attacks to come. Most of them are quite unaware afterwards that they've done it. And yet, in time trialling, where all you need is a fast rolling rhythm and no acceleration, the lowest – or anyway the least high – gears seem to be ridden not by the short-distance men but by the 100-milers and above.

If I go back to Norman Sheil again, for I respect his opinion greatly, I find that he wrote this in 1966;

> The other day somebody asked me why I was so anti-gear in time trials. The point is, I'm not. Neither am I anti-time trial. In fact, I don't think I'm anti-anything. If a rider wants to use a gear of 100 plus, who am I to stop him?
>
> What does upset me, however, is the fact that riders will blindly follow fashion without thinking what they are doing and why they are doing it, and this to me is very wrong. The fact that riders have accepted the idea that big gears are the answer to fast times would indicate that they are still looking for the magic formula to success – the easy way.
>
> First of all, if a rider wants to use a gear of 100 inches or more, he must realise that this entails primarily a strength exercise, and should be treated as such. Few people would be foolish enough to attempt anything that requires a greater strength than they possess, yet bike riders do it every week.
>
> Quite honestly, I would like to see a rider properly trained with the sole object of using big gears for time trialling. The result, I know, would put the whole problem in its right perspective and riders would immediately realise that there is more to this game than meets the eye.
>
> He would produce his sub-50 minute '25', not necessarily on a moat morning and a super-fast course, but on any reasonable course and decent morning. Now this to me is sense; blindly following other people's techniques (for this is all they are) is wrong.

Unless you use real mammoth gears, or by chance you find that you'd actually go faster on something smaller, the gear you use is not much more than the combination of your training, your skill and your technique, divided by the wisdom with which you chose that gear in the first place.

Most riders *do* use higher gears in time trials than they do in road races or pursuits. That much makes sense. But the further you go along that route, the more specialised you inevitably become as a time triallist. And there's nothing wrong with that, if that's what you want to be, although it's a physiological cul-de-sac which can shut you off from being very much else. Road and even track men have done remarkably well in time trials – the national road champion once also went on to win the BBAR as an afterthought in three straight rides, something unheard of before or since in time-trialling circles – but the feat has never been achieved the other way round. There are no time-trial specialists on the Continent as there are here, but even so it's fair to point out that the professionals who become feared against the clock were already pretty nifty in a bunch.

12 Pushing and twiddling

If time trialling is primarily a skill and endurance sport, and frankly that's what it is, then the obvious way to train is with a high proportion of long-to-medium intervals and a smaller share of speed work and bunch riding. The higher the gear you want to push, the greater becomes the strength and power angle.

To be honest, I don't see any pressing need for a gear much into the hundreds for most riders. The effective size of a gear is relative to your speed, of course – coming down a mountainside at 50 mph would make anything seem small – so logic says that the faster you ride, the larger the gear you need. The mistake comes in applying the argument the other way round; using a larger gear doesn't necessarily mean you'll go any faster. It may very well make you go slower.

I'm not a fanatic for low gears by any means. I think it's very easy to go too far in one direction as it is in another. But it's very odd to hear experienced club riders tell you 'I don't stand a chance of getting under the hour without a 110' when you know very well that even moderate riders were doing it on 86-fixed several decades ago.

The greatest campaigner for small gears I ever knew was an eccentric but well-meaning old coach called Peter Valentine, who'd shower every coaches' meeting with neatly duplicated examples of his argument.

I did once try it on someone with moderate success. I did it because the reasoning was so supremely logical and persuasive, but I abandoned it because it was also oppressively dull. It is, though, the only real schedule I've ever come across for time trialling, so I pass it on. It's based on the argument that an increase of gear produces more work but no guarantee of more speed, and depends therefore on the logic that pedal rate should be maintained as gears are increased. The gear sizes are ones chosen for schoolboys.

It runs like this: take your best 10-mile time and deduct a tenth. That'll mean an improvement of just more than two minutes unless you're abnormally slow. The new time is your ultimate target and the calculations (time trialling is a mathematical sport) are based on that and a schoolboy block.

Decide on a top gear – say 81 – and four descending gears. They might be 76.2, 72, 68.2 and 64.8. With a calculator you can find the number of pedal revolutions needed to reach your target in top gear. The formula is:

$$\frac{20160 \times 10 \text{ (which is the distance in miles)}}{\text{gear} \times \text{time in minutes}} = \text{pedal revs a minute}$$

The ideal pedalling speed in top gears, Valentine argued, is 105 revs a minute for distances up to 25 miles, 100 for 50 miles. Maximum pedalling, and then only in short bursts, is between 135 and 150, so 105 is far from outrageous.

Start with the bottom gear and aim to pedal at least a minute faster than the target pedalling speed. If your target is 105 in top gear, for example, decide on 117. This will take care of the lower resistance of the smaller gear. You can then work out the time you must beat by pedalling at 117 revs a minute in your bottom gear of 64.8. The formula is:

$$\frac{20160 \times 10}{\text{gear} \times \text{revs}} = \text{time in minutes}$$

Work out the target speed for each gear, reducing the pedalling speed by three revs a minute for each higher gear. On that schoolboy block it would mean:

64.8 at 117 rpm
68.2 at 114
72   at 111
76.2 at 108
81   at 105 = your ultimate target for 10 miles

Try using the gears flat out over two stretches of five miles, or even four of 2½ miles. Use an RTTC course for accuracy, preferably one where the start and finish are opposite each other, or modify one for your own purpose. Failing that, borrow a cyclometer, check it on a measured course (remember to use 27-inch wheels and not sprints, which are slightly smaller) and then measure out a course of your own nearer home. Don't rely on a cyclometer alone.

Have a short ride to warm up, then ride as fast as you can over five miles and time yourself. Stop at the turn to regain your breath, then race back to the finish. Add the two times (or the four times if you used a 2½-mile section) and compare the total to the target time for the gear. Try again on separate occasions until you match or beat the time.

Once you can manage it in one gear, go straight to the next, but never skip a gear even if the difference in time or pedalling rate is small. You'll see that, following the rule that training must be progressive to produce results, you never increase your gear in this tempo training until it will bring an increase in speed. That rule must apply to any change of gear, whether it's from tiny to not-so-tiny, or from enormous to colossal, Valentine argued. In the end – and in his experience very quickly – the gear did go up and the time did come down, and I suppose you could apply the principle indefinitely.

I used to sympathise with Peter Valentine because his argument was so sound, and his own successes so real, and yet every time one of his protegés turned up well in the national schoolboy '10' championship, it was always second to some big-gear thumper who thought the progressive gear theory was a load of old chutney. To be fair, though, many of Valentine's riders lasted longer than the big-gear riders who beat them.

Perfect your pace judging, if you wish, by riding briskly over a set distance, timing how long it takes. Now ride a mile or so further, turn and try to re-cover the whole return distance in the same time. Try, too, to ride out with the wind and get as near to your outward time when you retrace into the wind.

Finally, here are a few tips that an old boss of mine, Mike Daniell, passed on in *Cycling*:

No part of a race can be easy. Even when you are going downhill with the wind, you must still remember to make it hurt. If you don't, you will have lost valuable seconds to someone with greater courage.

Never lose heart on the hard stretches. Everyone will have a dose of the creeps there, tell yourself, and smash away that bit harder; never sit up.

Remember the Road Time Trials Council measurers define routes to the shortest way they can be legitimately ridden. There are no prizes for riders doing the best '26' or '51'.

Be wary at the dead turn in the road. There is a tendency to ease. Fight it off and hammer right up to the marshal. On gears, nick down into a suitable gear for accelerating away from the turn just before freewheeling round.

13 Timetable of success

By now it should all be wonderfully clear. You know what kind of rider you are and what you would like to be; you know what the particular demands are of your own section of the sport; you know what sort of training produces which kinds of results. All you need now is blinding inspiration to shuffle the whole lot into the right order.

The bit of paper that lists that order is called a training schedule. Other sports are very familiar with training schedules and training won't start without one. Bike riders, on the other hand, are a rebellious lot and not too keen on doing what other people tell them. But this schedule isn't anybody telling you to do anything. You've seen the arguments and you can decide for yourself. The schedule you draw up doesn't come like a demand from the tax office. It's not like the homework you get from school. It's something you decide for yourself.

I always think it's a bit like making jam. Everything you stuff into the bottle you can scoop out afterwards. If you don't put enough in, it runs out early.

Schedules are essentially individual and what one rider needs rarely suits another. That's why my old trick of following other people's training routines didn't do any good. To take extremes, it would be futile for a 6 ft 2 in coal miner doing shift work and having an interest in time trials trying to follow a schedule drawn up for a student of 5 ft 2 in who intends to ride only kermesses. Both ride a bike, but the similarity ends there.

Consider what you want before you commit yourself. What do you want to do this season? Which events do you want to do well in — this can mean more than winning. Is there a club championship you'd like, or simply a rival you'd like to beat? Be ambitious but be realistic. There's not much chance of being covered in mud and flowers at the end of Paris–Roubaix if the best you've managed previously was an equal seventh in a junior road race.

You can achieve whatever reasonable target you set yourself. You can get a second-cat licence if you're a third; you can knock several minutes off a '25' time; you could get a medal in the division pursuit championship. It's possible, and it depends on you.

Think of what you've done already and what you've got available.

(a) Spare time for all forms of training.
(b) The roads in your area and their suitability for speed and endurance training.
(c) A friend or coach to help generally.
(d) A gym for circuit and weight training.
(e) Space at home for mobility exercises, or perhaps weight training, or a set of rollers.
(f) The equipment you have.
(g) The hours that you work.
(h) The help you get from your parents, friends and most important, your coach (because by now you should have found one from the lists published by the BCF and RTTC).

Now start thinking of the next two months, and draw yourself up a diary. Mark off all the dates you know won't be available, and a day a week for recuperation or as a spare date when the weather forces a change of plan. Now look at the circle of training again and judge what you need, and what you can do. Mark in the weight-training and circuit-training days as appropriate.

Mark in the basic steady-state mileage if it's that time of year. Think of up to 2,000 basic miles if you're a senior riding long races; 1,500 miles for seniors riding conventional races; 500 miles for juniors; about the same for schoolboys, except the very youngest or tiniest.

Work out the progression you need and the mileages. Make sure your training gets harder as you get fitter and as the weather improves. Will you get to the standard of fitness you'd like by your first race? If not, should you start training earlier in the winter, or could you regard your first event(s) as training? In any case, to maintain progression, don't include a race simply because it's there; better to miss it than to start racing too early.

Later in the year, mark in the important races and the less important ones. Build your races round your training and not the other way about, or you'll start most of your races ill-prepared.

Work in the interval-based techniques in rough proportion to what is needed. Turn back a few chapters and look again. The higher the figure under 'speed', the more speed work you need. The more important the cruising, the more the advanced steady-state training, but everybody needs both.

The progression and the intensity of training can't continue indefinitely. By mid-season your standard of racing will be at its peak, and with it your training. Switch away from concentrated specialised training and into what the Swedes call 'fartlek' training, which translates best as speed play.

To the Swedes, it meant running through the woods, chasing rabbits, ambling along, jumping over a gate, sprinting again, and doing whatever they chose just for the fun of it, provided the intensity was there. That's why fartlek training is marked 50–50 on the speed–endurance ratings.

You can do the same on your bike, going out with a group, sprinting for signs, racing up hills and doing whatever you can to make the whole business both very tough and enjoyable.

If you have a second peak in the season, you can rebuild from this fartlek period suitably refreshed and even rested; always remember that rest is an important part of a schedule as well. The main difference between amateurs and professionals is that the professionals have, or ought to have, more time to rest.

Keep a diary all through your training and racing. Write in the training that you planned to do and what you actually managed. Write in any late or early nights, any minor illnesses or visits to the dentist – anything that might build up a pattern that you can recognise later. Next winter you'll be able to look back and see whether there was any identifiable thread which'll help you know yourself better.

Never be satisfied with your standard; always aim to improve it. At first the progress will be rapid as you take up the slack. Later it will be harder to maintain, and in the end it will stop or even decline as age takes over. But, well, you've seen the figures. Bike riders live to a grand old age and a lot of them go faster in their dotage than they did in their teens. Experience is a wonderful thing.

Experience will also show you when you're training too hard or too much. Some people regard it as staleness, or chronic fatigue, or just that they're fed up. It's usually overtraining. It's dreadful when it happens – all your drive goes, your morale falls, you get bored and you feel nervous.

It happens when you ask more of yourself than overadjustment can cope with. A small and progressive overload brings an improvement, but do too much and you're straining yourself, in the most general terms, and you start going backwards. One of the world's top running coaches said his athletes used to notice some or all of these symptoms:

— less general resistance, with headaches, sniffles, fever blisters etc.
— mild leg soreness which occurred from day to day (this is in runners, remember)
— an 'I don't care' attitude towards training and even quite everyday activities
— wanting to pack in races
— a kind of 'hangover' feeling from the previous race and a significant drop in body weight from the day before.

Doctors can tell all sorts of things from your blood, but you can't go running to a doctor every time you feel stuffed and you wonder whether there's more than the obvious reason for it. And even if you did, most doctors are much more used to dealing with the sick, not with very fit athletes who've got nothing clinically wrong with them. Their general answer if you tell them cycling hurts more than it used to is 'Well, stop cycling, then.' And who can blame them?

So, doctors are out. But the blood's still there, so maybe there's something to be learned from your pulse and heart rate. And indeed there is, except it's not terribly reliable.

Whenever you give yourself a good hammering, you recover in three stages. First, you get over the oxygen debt. Second, you get over the immediate stage of fatigue. But, third, it takes hours or even days to recover *completely* and in all that time your pulse will be ticking away faster than usual.

If you want to take this further, take your pulse rate before you get out of bed in the morning, before even you sit up. Count the beats for 15 seconds. Then count again right after you get up. Do this every day for a week, when you don't suspect any overtraining, and note the average difference between the two pulse rates.

While the difference stays more or less the same, you've got nothing to worry about. But if the difference increases suddenly it's a sign that you haven't got over the previous day's training.

The problem is that you can't take this as any more than a general guide, because it's so easy to get it wrong. It's easy to take your pulse at a slightly different time each morning; it's easy to get the figure slightly wrong; even the anxiety of worrying whether you've overtrained, and what result the pulse test will show, will be enough to alter your pulse rate. So don't be unnecessarily alarmed. Certainly don't over-react.

Americans are dead keen on all this sort of thing. In fact, they seem to get keener on all the fads and sciences in direct proportion to their un-keenness for hard training. You don't seem to hear the best riders harping on about it very much.

Audrey McElmury, the woman who set off the big American revival by winning the world road-race championship, reckons:

> We've heard many people say that they wouldn't train on a particular day because their pulse rate was high. They think this is a result of not being fully recovered from the previous day's training. This may be true, but unfortunately this variation can be due to a multitude of other external things. These may include staying up late, anxiety, sleeplessness, etc.
>
> What happens on race day if your pulse is up (or on any other day)? We feel that you should continue to train unless there are other bodily symptoms indicating being run down or sick. Pulse, if used as a sole indicator of when you can train, can be very misleading, and should be only one of the factors to consider about your physical state.

And I'll say 'Amen' to that.

Still, it can happen. Bob Addy, the former Tour de France rider, used to say that every rider had an energy cube inside him. Everyone had so much resistance to exercise, anxiety and general running about. What you used up on one, you didn't have left for the other. And whenever he went on winter training weekends with young riders, he'd harp on at them about energy cubes when he saw them running up and downstairs needlessly (bring everything down in one trip) or running around fretting about their bikes (it's still much as you last saw it).

You get much the same view in a book entitled *The Stress of Life*. The only way out, Hans Selye reckons there, is either to reduce your training or reduce the other things in life that are causing you stress.

If it catches up with you before you can remedy the causes, it could take some while to get out of it. That's the main difference between overtraining and simply feeling naturally tired or momentarily dis-spirited. The only cure for overtraining is simply to gear right down in life, and the worse the problem the more you need to slow up.

That's why I said at the outset that you have to draw up a realistic schedule for yourself. You have to build up all through your training and you have to recognise when you're at a natural peak so that you can switch into high-quality but less structured and more enjoyable training to sustain it.

The chances of overtraining are much reduced if you have a fair but not excessive amount of stamina training at the start of the winter, with a base of circuit and weight training. Sleep is a natural antidote to stress, so aim to get plenty of it and in regular amounts each night. Sleep's something hardly anybody knows much about, or why some people need more than others, but it's certainly true that the more stressful your training, the more you'll need to sleep afterwards.

One of the benefits of being a professional is that your life as a bike rider is much more under your control. Not only can you train more, but you can rest more as well. Many of the best amateurs have discovered that they can't compete at the standard which the sport's reached without also living the same way. I've even heard a team selector saying that he deliberately picked riders – amateurs – who had no job, because only they, he reasoned, would have had the time to train (and to rest) at the necessary level.

This isn't an encouragement to give up your job or your schooling in favour of bike riding. That would be a foolish thing to do under most circumstances. But it does show how important are regular sleep and regular meals.

14 Women and children first...

Most bike riders are men of over 18 years of age, so the sport is designed by and large for them. Juniors and, even more, schoolboys ride tailored versions of senior competitions. Legislation protects them, or at least it does what the rule-makers think ought to be done, because – as I said before – all the research that I've seen shows that the better juniors are at no physiological disadvantage when they ride directly against seniors.

The only difference for young riders is in their development. Weight training has to be more carefully devised to exclude exercises which use a lot of weight in general and a lot of weight on the spine in particular. And, as Peter Travers argues, training should include less or, he would say, close to no interval training, which would thicken the heart.

But what about women? For some reason, the whole sport seems to go overboard to put them in a class of their own. Their road races are kept short – even at world-championship level – but they can ride time trials as long as they wish.

Women have been kept out of all sorts of sports for years, for no very good reason. There was one theory, for example, that they couldn't cope with heat stress for long periods.

The truth is that there are differences between men and women – proportion of body fat, the number of red blood corpuscles, and the size of lungs and so on – but that women and men respond to training in the same way. Therefore, as has been realised with sports such as running, there are reasons why men and women cannot compete equally, but there's no reason why they shouldn't compete in events of the same length or intensity.

A good deal of the present situation stems, I'm sure, from the view of Victorian athletes that women need to be cossetted and protected, although quite from what nobody seems very sure.

Mandy Jones, Britain's world road-race champion at Goodwood, had no hesitation when I asked her whether women's races should be shorter or longer: 'No . . . for heaven's sake no more short races. Put the distances up.'

In sporting terms, the most remarkable differences are not those between the sexes – because they're well enough known already – but between the women themselves.

The most immediate consideration is the monthly menstrual cycle, and it affects many women differently. Some have no trouble with their periods whether they're racing or not. Others find their periods more troublesome than usual, while others have no periods at all.

Having no period at all – a condition known as secondary amenorrhea – was first heard of in long-distance runners. It seemed to be less connected with the exercise itself than with the 'thinness' of the girls concerned. It was to do with their low total body weight and the small amount of fat on their bodies, so the reasoning went. And the theory was underlined by the fact that the same thing happens with medically underweight hospital patients.

At the start of America's biggest international stage race in 1979, it turned out that one in eight of the women questioned had stopped menstruating during the season. They were training between 200 and 300 miles a week.

I've never seen any suggestion that this is harmful. In fact, apart from the apparent connection with low fat levels, there's no strong link between cycling and the cessation of menstruation.

Any bike rider knows that once you start training seriously, all sorts of things happen in your life as well as the frequency of your exercise. You may change what you eat, how much you sleep and when you sleep. You may worry more, or spend more time travelling. All these things can affect the hormones which control menstruation. They may restrict the hormones, or they may increase them. And so it's impossible to say whether cycling is *the* cause or whether it's just one of the causes of the cessation of menstruation.

Mysterious, isn't it? If you find that cycling lessens your period pains, there's no guarantee that more cycling will lessen them further. Nor will it necessarily make the pains greater. It's even a reasonable guess that bike riders accustomed to pain, as all athletes are, might be able to cope better with period pains.

The amount of research into this subject is very small – practically non-existent. Part of the trouble is that since menstruation problems vary so much from woman to woman, research would need to start *before* a girl became a bike rider (which would be difficult in the extreme, since it requires predicting the future) and continue long afterwards.

All the presently available evidence, however, shows that endurance sports *are* connected with menstrual difficulties, even with the temporary absence of menstruation, but that the connection isn't total. In the same race, you might well have some female riders suffering less from their periods, some suffering more, and some who've stopped menstruating completely.

The one obvious piece of advice is that, if you stopped menstruating at about the same time as you started racing or increased your training, do see your doctor but emphasise to him that the increased exercise should be considered.

15 Food for thought

There was this dotty idea going about at one time that tomatoes were bad news. Out in the American backwoods they called it the devil's fruit and heaven knew what would happen to anyone who ate one. Then some young daredevil stood on the steps of Salem County courthouse and astonished a crowd by wolfing a whole one. Only when he stayed upright did the people of Salem County come to see the tomato in a different light.

Some bike riders are like that. I don't suppose there's anything except water that I haven't heard one bike rider or another say was bad for cyclists. The fact is, there is nothing, short of being poisonous, that's actually bad for you. And almost everything is pretty good and doesn't need to be tampered with or added to. I am thinking in particular of a friend who cannot sit down to a meal without surrounding himself with an array of phials and bottles. Now the whole family's got the habit and every mealtime they all have a good shake, swallow and swill.

Health food shops and the whole-food movement have made the situation worse. Oh, I don't disagree with their aims. I think they're entirely on the right track and I wish them well. But where they go wrong is that they create an expensive paranoia about food which is to nobody's benefit but their bank manager's.

The truth is that, with one possible exception, there are adequate vitamins, protein and other nutrients in the typical European diet. The only difference between a bikie and an office worker is that the cyclist needs to eat more.

The food you eat must balance the energy you expend. If you eat too much, the balance is stored as fat. Eat too little and the body turns to its fat reserves to make up the difference. And if you eat seriously too little, like slimmers who get carried away with the idea, the body gobbles up all the fat and then starts work on the muscles.

There's no bad food, not even junk food. Not even Big Macs with relish. All food has nutritional value. The knack lies in getting a balanced diet, not one which has an unusual dependence on Mars bars, Carling Black Label and Wimpyburgers.

You can divide food into two main classes; the first produces or stores energy, and the other builds and repairs. Sugar and fat are the energy foods while proteins, which are contained in meat, eggs and cheese, build and repair your muscles and other working parts.

Immediately, though, you need energy and primary energy – in other words, energy that doesn't rely on what happens when you go into oxygen debt – comes from sugar. It comes from carbohydrates and other food that the body breaks down. The first stage of this breaking-down process happens within moments of your putting food into your mouth, the moment that the saliva gets to work on it.

Potatoes, for example, may contain little sugar in their raw state, but they do contain starch and starch breaks down into maltose, which is a kind of sugar. Potatoes, therefore, are a source of energy.

Rather unfairly but with a hint of truth, advertising and women's magazine features brand carbohydrates as fattening. They're not, not automatically. If you get fat through eating carbohydrates, it's your fault. If you eat more than you need, you store the surplus as fat beneath your skin and inside your muscles. Both are a handicap in bike racing. If your weight remains stable, you can be sure that you're not eating too much sweet food.

Fat is also a source of energy, but it's not as good as sugar. It's a reserve force which you can't use until you've worked your way through a lot of the sugars. Until then it wobbles about, unused and usually unwanted. There doesn't have to be much of it before it becomes a serious disadvantage, first because the fat globules act as friction pads inside your muscles, and second because it's just that much more weight that you've got to hike uphill with you.

At the start of a training ride, you use sugars; after about four to six hours, you use more and more fat, and longer rides like that will train your body to use fat more efficiently.

Every time you move, you wear yourself down a little. The working parts come under stress and then relax again, the joints wear against each other, the bones come under tension. To make the necessary repairs, you need the food from which muscles are made – protein. There are thousands of possible combinations of the amino acids that constitute protein and the whole subject is bewilderingly complicated. Fortunately most of the amino acids will change from one type to another as the body demands. The two main proteins in muscle are actin and myosin.

Eight of the amino acids, though, are stubborn. *They won't change.* They're crucial to your continued health so, not surprisingly, they're called the essential amino acids. Their names – although you needn't remember them – are rather splendid: isoleucine, leucine, phenylalanine, lysine, valine, tryptophan, methionine and threonine. You get them especially from meat, eggs and cheese, and they're called first-class proteins.

There's a double problem here for vegetarians. You get both carbohydrate and protein from a vegetarian diet, but most vegetables lack at least one of the essential amino acids. A protein supplement could well be needed.

The other problem for vegetarians is that they often have trouble keeping up their weight. You very rarely see a fat vegetarian, simply because their food typically lacks any quantity of carbohydrate. More than that, it contains a lot of fibre, which makes the intestine and bowel work that much faster. It's certainly true that vegetarians seem to spend more time either eating or using the lavatory. In fact, the digestive process can work so quickly for a vegetarian that at times the body doesn't have time to extract all the proteins with which it's presented.

However, there have been too many first-class athletic performances by vegetarians to suggest that a no-meat diet is unsuitable or even dangerous, but you need to take a lot more care over supplements.

Vegetarian diets also lack one of the smallest of the vast range of vitamins – B_{12}. Vitamins are pretty much newcomers to the nutrition scene. A Polish chemist called Casimir Funk discovered what turned out to be a vitamin just before the First World War. The poor chap wasn't certain what he'd turned up, but he had a pretty good idea that it was essential to life (*vita*) and that it was an amine. (The years have removed the final e from vitamine.)

Funk had the idea that his new find would cure beri-beri. He was wrong but his discovery triggered off some of the most intensive research for centuries. To start with, the scientists gave each vitamin an identifying letter. Then they found some vitamins had sub-groups, so they talked of vitamins B_1 and B_2 and so on. Then they discovered they'd filled up the alphabet and they were still finding more, so they're in All Sorts Of Trouble, as David Coleman would say.

All the vitamins in a group are like each other, but hugely different from vitamins of a different letter. The only thing they have in common is that all vitamins are catalysts – they don't do anything themselves, but their presence makes other things possible.

There's a lot of myth surrounding vitamins. They're still so recent, in medical terms, that scientists are finding out more and more about them all the time. And what the scientists don't know, there are plenty of people willing to fill in with guesswork and supposition.

There is, though, an undeniable link between vitamins and athletic performance. So what *is* known about them?

Well, vitamins B and C dissolve in water, while others don't. This is important because it means you can store most vitamins but you have to have a daily intake of B and C, the excesses of which get flushed away. We know that the B group is tied in with the way you extract energy from food, and that C prevents scurvy and helps mend strains and wounds.

Just as important, we know that C is damaged by heat. And since it comes in vegetables such as brussels sprouts, which are cooked before being eaten, you can see that a lot of the vitamin gets destroyed by the heat or dissolved in the water that you throw down the drain. Fortunately, vitamin C is also found in oranges and in potatoes. Therefore, if you eat sensibly you should never suffer a vitamin C deficiency. A normal portion of boiled cabbage contains more vitamin C than five times the amount of lettuce. Blackcurrants, rose hip syrup and parsley are all rich in vitamin C, but apples come low in the league.

Fortunately, vitamin B is less cantankerous. There are many forms, usually identified with a number, B_6, or with a name – riboflavin – or with both a name and a number. All the B group are concerned with ensuring that you extract energy from your food. One of them, B_{12}, goes a long way to preventing pernicious anaemia. We'll look at that again in a moment because, being the latest to be discovered and unique in that it contains a metal, it has a mythology of its own.

The first of the B group, B_1, is the one most closely connected with energy. Doctors who looked at a group of Australian athletes decided that they should all be taking in more B_1, or thiamine as it's known. Assuming that it takes 0.4 mg of thiamine to process 1,000 calories of food (a calorie is a measurement of the heat or energy potential of a food), an inactive man consuming 2,500 calories will need 1 mg of thiamine. An athlete eating 4,000 calories will need half as much again (1.6 mg) and a stage race rider whose calorie intake is formidable will take still more.

Thiamine is fortunately a common vitamin. You find it in liver

(0.3 mg), cod's roe (1.5), flour (0.28–0.4), eggs (0.1) and bacon, pork and ham (0.3). (The proportions are to 100 gm of the particular food.) If you work it out, you'll see that a normal diet will contain sufficient thiamine and that all you need do is eat more of the relevant foods in order to obtain the thiamine to cope with the increased calorie intake. Bread, for example, contains flour and therefore thiamine, so a slice of bread (thiamine) and jam (carbohydrate) is a good energy source.

If you're really concerned, you can buy vitamin B tablets at a chemist's or health food shop. The surplus will just be flushed away. The same applies to vitamin C.

The other vitamins in the B group will often substitute for thiamine. The one stranger in the collection is B_{12}. As promised, we'll look at it again when we come to the subject of anaemia.

All the other vitamins are needed in fairly small quantities. It's not a good idea to supplement them because you store them in your fat and too much can give you hypervitaminosis. It's bad enough having to pronounce it, so heaven knows what the symptoms are.

Vitamin E is a health shop favourite because scientists discovered that it makes rats randy. So it's sold now in the form of rejuvenating cream and even as a fertility drug.

In Russia, where they're dead keen to test everything possible on their athletes, they gave varying doses of vitamin E to 34 cyclists and skiers. They tested their blood pressure and their urine and they decided that those with the largest doses did best. But the results were only experimental and far from generally accepted, and taking too much vitamin E can produce high blood pressure.

Compared to vitamins, minerals get hardly any publicity at all. There are so many of them, for one thing, and most of them are present in the body in the right amounts. The most important of the minerals is iron, and iron is all to do with anaemia.

There are something like five grams of iron in your body, about enough to make half a dozen paper clips. They're distributed in three main kinds of compound of which the largest and most important is haemoglobin.

It is haemoglobin that gives blood its red or purple colour. Its function is to carry oxygen round the body. Haemoglobin itself travels around the blood, which is mainly water, in minute bi-concave discs called corpuscles. You can get an idea of the size of the things if you remember that there are ten pints of blood inside you and that those ten pints carry five million red cells in each cubic millimetre of blood. Each *single* red cell contains 280 *million* molecules of haemoglobin. Each haemoglobin molecule contains 10,000 atoms of hydrogen, carbon, oxygen and sulphur – and just four atoms of iron. How can something so minute be of such great importance to the way you race?

Iron's like the octane rating of petrol when you are the racing car. If there's enough iron, you go fast. If there's too little, you don't go so well. When there's too little iron in the blood, the condition's called anaemia, and in athletes it's very bad news.

Normally each red cell lives for six weeks. Then it falls apart and sheds iron, some of which the body keeps and the rest of which it excretes. The system changes in athletes such as cyclists, though. More than the usual amount of iron is lost and so the blood's more likely to become anaemic, or weak. When doctors tested British cyclists before the Tokyo Olympics, they found most were anaemic.

As a cyclist, you're more prone than usual to anaemia because the speed at which the blood travels round the body destroys the weaker cells faster than normal. This doesn't happen all the time, for some reason. It's likely to happen at the start of a training season, or when you're tired or unfit. The stronger cells survive for six weeks, but the others last for only two or three, so you lose more iron than usual. After that, it's even possible that your blood becomes stronger than usual, although it could still weaken suddenly and inexplicably. It's reasonable to suppose this happens when you notice the signs of over-training, because the symptoms of both conditions are very similar:

- breathlessness
- pins and needles in hands or feet
- sudden fall-off in racing results
- headaches and insomnia
- sudden loss of enthusiasm, or an inability to train.

If you suspect anaemia, you should check with your doctor straight away. He can arrange a blood test, or even carry out a simple test on the spot.

Vitamin B_{12} does have a connection with the prevention of certain kinds of anaemia, notably pernicious anaemia, but the amounts needed are minute and its role is far from clear. Certainly if you've got any hint of pernicious anaemia, you're much more of a hospital case than a racing cyclist.

The vitamin is often injected in large amounts on the Continent (but then so's a great deal else). Peter Travers reckoned:

There is no reliable evidence that B_{12} has any effect on human performance, and certainly none that is necessary for normal health, provided that a normal, balanced diet is given.

I think that one can really discount the slender evidence from the world of professional cycling, since their dietary and drug intake has no rational basis at all. In the world of amateur cycling a much more sane approach is developing.

I am afraid that there is no evidence to suggest that injections of B_{12} would help athletes in any way at all, provided that they were taking a normal balanced diet. Indeed, there is some evidence that excessive doses of some vitamins could well be harmful . . .

We know that hard training does bring about iron deficiency and is rapidly corrected by taking organic iron – something like Ferrograd C – but even here it is as well to establish by doing a blood test, and then to control the amount of iron by giving serial tests, rather than giving iron wholesale.'

Ferrograd C is very effective. It can make you constipated, but it works quickly. They're long red tablets, a bit like red beans. Take them as the instructions advise, but not for more than three days at a time without a break. A lot of doctors think that if you keep taking iron tablets, the body gets out of the habit of extracting iron from food. In the end, the argument runs, you might become dependent, at least for a while, on artificial iron. And you can see from Peter Travers' comment that just taking it wholesale to be on the safe side isn't a good idea.

If you think you're anaemic and iron tablets don't make you feel better within a few days, see your doctor.

Smoking will make your blood less efficient at picking up oxygen. As few as ten inhalations of tobacco smoke can cause a huge reduction in the amount of air that can be drawn in. Smoking upsets the way that oxygen and haemoglobin link together in the blood and it could therefore deplete your energy. Smoking can also upset your nervous system and make your heartbeat ragged and irregular.

All that and the links with cancer as well! It makes you wonder why *anybody* smokes, doesn't it?

16 Drink and drugs

It's said that we head for the coast each summer because we're made largely of water. It's everywhere, but it's particularly in the blood. In fact, blood is almost entirely composed of water and that's what makes it flow.

You may have around six litres of blood and while you're not doing anything in particular it moves round at about five litres a minute. Once you start riding really hard, it circulates at up to 30 litres a minute.

Exercise at that level produces a lot of heat, and consequently you sweat to keep the heat down. The sweat is water produced by the kidneys and, after a while, by the blood itself. Luckily, bike racing is a fast-moving sport, so the wind does a lot to help reduce sweating. But on a particularly hot day, the body is under dual attack, being heated from the inside and from the outside.

If you lose a lot of water through sweating, you end up with thicker blood or even less blood than before. And that, of course, initially affects your performance, continues until you suffer from dehydration, and ends in death.

It was dehydration which made Jim Peters collapse on the track within yards of the finish of the Commonwealth Games marathon at Vancouver. You've maybe seen that famous piece of archive film. And it was dehydration, brought on by drugs, that killed Tom Simpson during the Tour de France.

Doctors don't agree on how often you should drink during a race, but they all seem to think you should swig something often. They seem puzzled by the common view that drinking fills the stomach and stops you eating and thereby taking in sugars. In fact, they say, if you don't have something to drink at intervals during even a one-hour race, the chances are you're reducing your performance.

Of course, it could well be that in a '10' or even a '25', it would take longer and be more disruptive to take a drink on the move than it would be to ignore it. That could well be, but you can see that frequent mouthfuls are important at 50 miles and more.

The blood flowing close to the skin helps keep the body cool in the way that a radiator keeps a car engine cool. But if fluid loss means less blood, your brain reacts by sending what blood is left to the more important areas like your muscles, ignoring more and more of the rest, like your skin. That starts a vicious circle because less blood on the skin surface means you have to sweat more to keep cool, and more sweating means less fluid available to keep your blood thin. And so it goes on.

The mildest forms of heat injuries include heat cramps, fainting – which is rare – and general heat fatigue. None of these is likely in normal European weather, but they're possible in a heatwave or in southern Europe.

Heat exhaustion is the most likely affliction. It causes extreme weakness, dizziness, headache, nausea and moist skin. Body temperature will remain almost normal, though, and the remedy is to get to a cool area and drink a lot of fluid, without guzzling it down all at once.

I don't want to panic you. None of this is likely in anything like normal conditions. But it does show that drinking during a race is important, doesn't it? The sensation of feeling thirsty comes rather later than the start of fluid shortage, so drink before you think you need it. Sip little and frequently.

If you still think that drinking during a race is harmful, try this test. Time yourself over a mile or two, come back home and drink as much water as you can, then time yourself over the same distance. There'll be no difference except a slight slopping sensation in your stomach.

The only rules to remember about drinking during events are: not too much, not too cold, and certainly not alcoholic or gassy. And certainly you should never be tempted to use the drink to swallow anything that you oughtn't.

Cycling is a sport that has been and probably still is riddled by a drugs problem. In British amateur cycling it's minimal but on the Continent, just as in other endurance sports, it's widespread. The only difference between the present time and the problem's peak in the Sixties is that riders are no longer falling over in races and dying on the spot.

This isn't the place to go into a long explanation, but basically there are two families of drugs which relate to cycling. The first – the stimulants – have been around for as long as sport has existed but came to an early peak when amphetamine was produced in great quantities during the Second World War.

Amphetamine, benzedrine and the rest produce great feelings of elation and concentration. They give you a buzzing feeling and make you think that everything you do is rather better than it is. In fact, the brain acts irrationally and riders drugged on amphetamine tend to talk occasional gibberish and in extreme cases have lost all self control, foaming at the mouth and smashing up their bikes.

The almost obsessive concentration that the drugs provide can sometimes let you drive yourself beyond the normal point at which the pain barrier would stop you. Tom Simpson was drugged on amphetamine and alcohol when he carried on riding on Mont Ventoux even though he had severe dehydration (something which the drugs would have made worse).

Stimulants like these work by improving just one part of your fitness, of your bodily machine. But fitness is a perfect symmetry, an optimum balance of all the body's different functions and improving one part and not the rest causes an imbalance. For this reason, riders who depend on stimulants have occasional good rides but a very patchy record. They also usually go into a slow but progressive decline.

Amphetamines – which are sold under many names – work directly on the brain and produce a quick dependence. Not only do you become paranoid, literally, about taking them but your tolerance increases and you have to take more and more to achieve the same effect.

Continued use can cause severe mental and other health problems. Their only benefit is *occasional* good results (although the doped rider invariably believes he has performed better than he has), against which have to be set erratic and worsening results and severe medical problems.

By the end of the Sixties, the sport had introduced more frequent and more efficient dope tests. Many prominent riders were caught and the emphasis changed from stimulants to body-building drugs.

Californian beachboys started using anabolic steroids many years ago and a doctor who at one time encouraged athletes to use them to build up their muscles soon changed his mind when he saw how out of control steroid abuse became and what the medical side-effects were. But by then it was too late.

Cyclists discovered steroids quickly but soon came to realise that the drugs in the cortisone group were more useful. Cortisone is a drug which the body uses to repair injuries and speed up recuperation.

Using them in sport, it was argued, was stimulant doping in reverse. If you couldn't take drugs *before* a race to make you go faster, why not take something *afterwards* to make you recover more quickly for the next day's race? Obviously this would be very useful in a stage race.

It didn't take someone very long to discover that a very large dose of cortisone not only helped recovery but acted as a stimulant as well. Whoopee! And the doctors, at that time, couldn't detect it.

Nobody knows for sure just what anabolic steroids do, although they're accused of producing partial or total sterility in men and partial sex changes (such as beard growth) in women. The side-effects of cortisone are already visible, though. Bernard Thevenet, who became a French hero after winning the Tour de France, withdrew dramatically and miserably from the sport and said cortisone was to blame. Other prominent and sudden departures have also been attributed to cortisone.

Taking cortisone, it seems, stops the body producing it for itself, or lessens its usefulness, with the result that quite minor injuries don't heal any more. Internal stresses, even problems caused by other drugs, no longer clear up.

There are a great number of drugs and allied substances and techniques prevalent in many sports, some of them plain dotty (like pumping air up swimmers' backsides to make them float better) and others really sinister. I suppose we are moderately fortunate in being an endurance rather than a strength sport and that, if cycling really put itself out, it could restrict the problem very much more, whereas the situation in the throwing sports is now almost out of control.

I shan't moralise. Moralising does no good. It may be that you will come up against doping at some time. If you're lucky, you'll just read about it. If you're unlucky, you'll try it. Don't consider it cheating. Just remember that it's ruined a great number of people in the past – even, or especially, riders with specialist advisers – and I don't suppose there's any reason that you'll be different.

17 Time, gentlemen, please

Bike racing takes up a lot of time. I was a swimmer when I was a kid and nothing was easier than turning up for a gala with nothing much more than a pair of swimming trunks and a towel. There were none of the routines that go with bike racing – looking for your number in the grass at the start of a time trial, signing on and getting your bike checked at a road race or track meeting. Nor were the races usually so far away from home.

Preparing for a race and travelling there are all part of the training, really. It's not just coincidence that the best riders never find themselves in the situation where they've left their shoes at home, or are stuck without arm warmers on a cold day, or can't find their crash hats. Good riders don't put embrocation on their legs and then use their oily fingers to put on their crash hats, thereby ensuring that a good sweat brings embrocation streaming into their eyes. They don't do things like that because they've got themselves sorted out.

Give yourself plenty of time. Get there an hour before a road race, three-quarters of an hour before a time trial (except on very cold mornings or if you've got an early start). Get straight out of your car when you arrive to avoid the nervous tiredness that many people feel. Keep fresh air coming into the car all through the journey.

Get all the paperwork sorted out first – the signing-on, the bike check, collecting your number and so on – and then get changed. Or, better still, get changed before you travel and get a friend to sort out the bike check for you. Save all your energy for riding – don't go running round the changing rooms.

If you're time trialling, get to the timekeeper a minute before you're due to start. Don't hang around there earlier but just circle gently in the road. Glance at where the numbers are kept and check whether the five riders ahead of you and the three behind you have all collected their numbers. At a road race, stay in the first ten all the time, even in the neutralised section. Make sure you know the finish stretch, particularly if it's off the circuit. Don't carry your car keys or money with you – they're very painful to fall on.

Always wear two jerseys – the first will slide on the second if you crash and the jersey will tear rather than your skin. Wear socks in a time trial – you've got to in a road race, anyway – for appearance and hygiene's sake. And always buy your training and race clothing for quality rather than sheer fashion.

Your preparations, of course, should include a warm-up. Now, there are about as many theories concerning warm-ups as there are sports boffins. So let's wade through what's known.

First of all, exercise raises the temperature, both on the surface, at your skin, and deeper inside you. Generally, your skin temperature will go up about ten degrees Fahrenheit and your inner or core temperature by about two degrees. And for every rise of a degree in body temperature there's a rise of about 13 per cent in muscle metabolism, better exchange of oxygen from the blood to the muscles, fibre contractions are both stronger and faster, and electrical messages from the brain travel along the nerves more quickly.

The build-up of exercise, even the anticipation of it when you're feeling nervous before the start, will also increase the flow of adrenalin into the blood, which in turn peps you up into a nervous state and gets your heart beating faster so that you can acclimatise to effort more quickly and accumulate an oxygen debt more slowly.

Nobody will deny, either, that muscles work better when they're warm. But does a muscle work hard *because* it's warm, or does it get warm simply because it's working hard? And, either way, does the average short warm-up before a race do enough to make an appreciable difference?

It takes something approaching half an hour's fairly intensive work to raise muscle temperature – if you're one of those roadmen who never feel comfortable on the first lap, that's probably why. Yet if you warm up long and hard, you'll be using up the very energy that you want for the race. Could, then, the energy you use in warming up be the energy that makes the difference between winning and losing?

Well, the truth – so far as it can be worked out – goes like this. The warm-up has to raise body temperature but not enough to create fatigue, so it's probably sufficient to raise a sweat and no more. And since that will take up energy, the warm-up should start to taper off about quarter of an hour before the race starts and finish completely with ten minutes still to go. The final gap before the race starts isn't too long because the benefits of a warm-up between 15 minutes and half an hour appear to last 30 minutes or more.

A warm-up also helps get your mental attitude straight, making you more determined and improving your co-ordination. If you can carry out a few simple stretching exercises about an hour before the start, the warm-up will be even more effective. After completing both the exercises and the warm-up itself, remember to wrap up warmly and not stand around in flimsy race clothing.

Bike riders don't usually suffer from muscle strains and joint injuries simply because cycling doesn't involve sudden, complete or even irregular movements. But at least you have the satisfaction of knowing that a good warm-up also makes the chance of injury even less likely.

The greatest difficulty with warming-up seems to occur where there is the greatest need for this preparation – in track races. It's in the nature of track promotions that every rider either has too great a gap between individual events or has three or four coming one after the other. This isn't necessarily the organiser's fault. It's just the way things happen. But it does nothing to make life easier for you and your warm-ups, nor does the fact that tracks are designed for racing on or sitting around, not for getting in some individual exercise.

I suppose there must be tracks somewhere where you can take a road bike and go for a brisk ride on the roads outside, but it's a risky business because the race may start without you. Luckily, more and more clubs now have sets of rollers, which are well worth taking to track races with you. Have your normal warm-up in the half-hour group session that precedes the meeting, then warm up again as necessary on the rollers according to the race timetable.

There's a current fashion of taking road bikes into the track centre and trundling about on them. If there are any advantages, they must surely be only mental. Gentle riding helps concentration and mental acuteness, but only if the trundling about doesn't involve tight cornering, variations in pace and anything approaching an obstacle course in and out among other riders and wandering officials.

Track centre riding on a road bike ought to be like going for a walk by yourself in a park, a time to be alone with your thoughts. Certainly there's no other benefit, other than that you'll be mildly warmer and less cramped than sitting about. The degree of exercise is nowhere enough to raise your inner temperature.

Hot showers, baths and massage can improve performance, but they've got nothing on exercise. Even a gentle jog is better than massage or a shower alone. A bike ride is best.

I refer again to Mike Daniell; he had this to say in *Cycling* all those years back:

> Experts at Loughborough have said that there is no physiological reason to warm up at all. My own view is that if they spent just a fraction of the time they give up to making these dogmatic statements in getting on with the job of going as fast between points A and B on a bike as they possibly could, we should get nearer the truth.
>
> For '25s' in my experience, a warm-up of at least eight miles is essential for the mature riders . . .

The crucial words, I suppose, are 'in my experience'. Nobody can produce the universal recommendation any more than he can draw up the universal training schedule. It's all a matter of trial and error based on sound general principles.

Mike's own method, by the way, he explained a few sentences later:

> On gears, I like to use about 75 inches at evens (20 mph). I would ride up the road in front of the start and follow an earlier starter at a respectful distance to get attuned to racing pace. Generally, provided you don't select a really top rider, this is quite reassuring as the rider can be held quite easily and this improves your morale.

The position about warm-ups has become clearer with more and more research and a more refreshing attitude over the years towards training and general race preparation. What's not a mite clearer, though, is whether bike riders should go on using such vast amounts of embrocation.

When I started, we had some terrible-smelling spirit in a bottle. Curacho, it was called, and the label told you it was what the champions used. It was thin, like water, smelled of ether or something like that, and even on freezing mornings along the Amersham road it would evaporate and disappear within seconds. I've no idea what good it did for us but, just like everything else, we used it because it was what all our mates used.

It stayed popular with us until someone discovered Musclor embrocation cream, which came with flashy diagrams of muscles and massage, and lots of French text, and had a smell like melting plasticine. There were also three grades so you could pretend you knew what you were doing by buying all three tubes. However, by then the market had exploded and there were so many brands available that we just went by what smelled most fashionable and smeared it on contentedly.

Embrocations come in different forms. Some are just a thick oil with various additives, and they're used to form a thin barrier between you and cold air. Others are irritants, which aggravate the skin and bring blood to just below the surface, making your leg (presumably) feel warmer. Others are a mixture of the two.

On top of that, any half-decent embrocation will also be reasonably fluid, or at least not too sticky, so that it can be used as a massage cream. In fact, so far as massage is concerned, you don't need a special embrocation at all, because all you're looking for is lubrication. Baby oil or olive oil will do the job perfectly well, and if you don't want to get sticky, even talcum powder will work.

The irritants – or, strictly, the counter-irritants – are something of a trick. By bringing the blood to skin level, they will indeed make your limbs feel warmer. But only on the surface, because, of course, they have to get the blood from somewhere and it comes from the muscle itself.

Still, a limb that *feels* warm is a great psychological bonus and by the time you've warmed up, the blood will be back in the muscle and you'll be glowing all over. The embrocation will then be acting more as a barrier against the cold. It does block the pores as well, I suppose, and it makes all manner of muck stick to you, but I've never heard anyone go into the evils of that.

Bike riders use more embrocation than any other group of athletes that I know of, and the makers are well aware of it. But then perhaps the need is greater because there can't be many sports in which athletes move through cold air at such a speed.

Dr Vaughan Thomas's conclusions were that faith could move mountains. If you think the embrocation helps, go ahead and use it. The psychological benefits will outweigh any physiological harm.

Do make sure you remove all of it afterwards, though. Eau-de-cologne, especially cheap eau-de-cologne in big plastic bottles, effectively does the job. And it makes people give you odd glances when you stop for a cup of tea on the way home, too.

Immediately after the race finishes, do remember to keep on riding. So many riders get to the line and stop almost dead, or drop dramatically into the grass verge, that you'd think competition records were falling every few minutes. It may look dramatic, you may feel knackered, but resist the temptation. There's lactic acid in your muscles and its dispersal is effected more easily if you keep riding gently.

Gentle cooling down is even more important at a track meeting because a sudden stop after one race, followed by a break and then more racing, is a good way of bringing on muscle stiffness.

18 Rashes and bashes

It's one of the great if sad truths of bike racing that we all fall off our machines now and again. Most of the world finds it quite amusing; just tell the folk at school or at work that you fell off on your way in and I guarantee that you'll raise more derogatory laughs than sympathy. Short of seeing someone slip on a banana skin, there's nothing in life more hilarious than a cyclist coming a cropper.

Unfortunately, it's very difficult to see the funny side of it when you're the one who's fallen off. And when you go flying at 20, 30 or even 40 mph, it gets progressively less amusing.

Fortunately, bike riding injuries are not often serious. Even broken bones are rare and the most spectacular crashes at the end of road races, ones in which half the field looks as though it must surely have died, end with everyone limping away with little more than gory but superficial cuts and grazes.

Collar bones can break, of course. And the skin on your knees and elbows can be dramatically thin. But in the end it just means another scar.

I remember treating a young rider who'd crashed on a course in Hertfordshire. He looked down at the side of his elbow and asked what the creamy white stuff under the cut could be.

'That?' I said. 'That's your bone.' And immediately I regretted it because news like that can be enough to produce shock or even panic. I needn't have worried. Bike riders are a phlegmatic lot, even at 16, and this lad's only reaction was mild interest and a muttered 'Oh, s'funny, innit?'

Fashions in first aid change almost yearly, and there's a marked difference between the first aid you need in sport, where you want to keep training and racing, and the kind that everybody else gets — bandage it up and keep it rested.

I bow to nobody in my general admiration for the enthusiasm and dedication of the St John Ambulance Brigade, but there are times when I've tried to stop riders falling into their care! St John members stand about all day waiting for somebody to practise on. They spend hours and hours in cold village halls learning their craft, and they're so keen that they buy all their uniforms, bandages and equipment themselves. So when the big moment comes, they wield the bandages with professional enthusiasm.

Actually, in the end there's very little you can do for your average cut or graze, anyway. If it needs stitching it's a hospital job and the most you can do at the roadside is stem the bleeding, and the St John brigade are at their best here.

Otherwise, treatment for ordinary injuries is a routine of stopping the bleeding, cleaning the wound, and preventing it from getting dirty again while nature takes its course. Luckily, a fit body responds well to an injury and heals fast.

Niagara falls; Gordon Singleton of Canada falls foul of Nakano of Japan.

There is an associated problem however, which should be mentioned. I refer to tetanus – but more of that in a moment.

Cuts and grazes clear up best when the air can get to them and if the pressure of blood is removed from the wound. Just use soapy water, or a mixture of water and disinfectant, to clear dirt from the wound – always work from the wound outwards, making sure that no dirty water runs back into the cut. Lift the limb so that gravity doesn't increase blood pressure to the site, mop up the blood until it starts to congeal, and then leave it.

There are various preparations you can buy (with some difficulty) which discourage bleeding by closing over the vein endings. They're a dramatic red colour, and hospitals don't like them at all. But, sensibly used, they're useful because they treat the wound without producing too much bleeding and too much of a clot.

A large blood clot, particularly on an extensive graze, can make subsequent training very painful. The fact that you're most likely to graze a joint, especially your knee, only makes it worse.

Blood clots form quite naturally and they're a hygienic seal against infection. 'Nature's own protection' is how they were described when I first learned first aid in the Scouts. Clots form most easily under a bandage and, in my experience, also if you treat the wound with one of the available antiseptic creams.

I'm a great believer in stemming the blood flow as quickly as possible, then mopping away what's left at intervals until only the thinnest smear of sticky blood remains. Then let the air get to the wound and resume training straightaway. In fact, gentle riding as soon as practicable after a crash will stop the area around the wound stiffening and causing further discomfort.

If the wound is too deep to treat fully by the roadside, don't hesitate to go to a hospital. Apply a non-stick dressing and a tightish but not stifling bandage to stem the flow, having cleaned the area as best you can. Leave the limb elevated and get a lift to the hospital. Note that it's generally quicker to get someone on the spot drive to a hospital than wait for an ambulance. You can obtain directions to the nearest hospital by dialling 999 and carefully explaining what you want. I say 'carefully' because many hospitals don't have functioning casualty departments on a Sunday or even at all.

The hospital staff will insist on administering an anti-tetanus injection. This is fairly logical because tetanus is a disease carried by animals and birds, deposited on country roads and easily transferred to human flesh, especially if the road is at all wet. It also kills within three days.

The injection lowers your susceptibility to infection, but it also lowers your general form. Now, form is something every athlete understands but can't define. It's also something that hospital nurses, under instructions from their doctor and busy enough already without having awkward bike riders for patients, have never heard of at all.

If you've had a full course of anti-tetanus injections and they're still valid, you can get out of having more at the hospital and still avoid dying. You do have to remember when you had the last jab, though, or you'll get another one 'just to be safe'.

In view of this, it is sensible to be prepared and have precautionary jabs – they're free – from your doctor during the winter. The loss of form will then occur when it matters least but the benefits will last for years.

Let us return to the subject of injuries. These might go deeper than the surface. The muscle tissue can be damaged by smacking against the road, for example. Or it can be strained by being unexpectedly stretched, again usually in a crash.

The treatment entails trying to disperse the swelling, which can appear quickly. The items that you need – bags of ice cubes – are, in the nature of life, the very things you don't stand a chance of having by you when you're racing. But, if you're desperate, pubs and private houses usually have at least a few ice cubes and a plastic bag. Or, failing that, use a cloth soaked in as cold a liquid as you can find.

Put the ice bag on the bruise or strain and keep it there for about half an hour. (Thereafter apply the cold compress twice a day.) Remove the ice bag, carefully, dry the bruise, and tie an elastic bandage moderately tightly round the affected area. Now, remember you're not trying to stop the blood flow. You're not trying to support a joint. So don't go OTT and have the limb dropping off through blood starvation. What you want is light compression to stop any more swelling or internal bleeding. Keep the limb upright, or at least raised.

Within a few hours, the damaged area will start turning spectacular colours. Don't worry, it's quite normal. Just keep on applying the ice pack twice a day until the inconvenience and pain have passed or the swelling has gone.

You can start racing again as soon as it feels comfortable.

A regular problem for any bike rider is a saddle boil. Everyone's had one; some riders get them more than others, and some get them far too frequently.

The small area of skin which comes between you and your saddle hasn't got much going for it, really. No one would say it was the most attractive part of the body. It's sweaty, it rarely sees daylight, and it's covered in hair follicles. Add to this the friction set up from movement on a narrow saddle and you can begin to understand the reasons for saddle boils.

An infection sets up, usually at a hair follicle, and pus builds up beneath the skin. In no time there's a boil which is further aggravated by the friction and the pressure. Generally these eruptions just come and go, but there have been cases of riders needing major and risky operations to get rid of huge boils which have spread themselves right around the groin.

Patrick Sercu, winner of more six-day races than anyone in history. But note the first-aid treatment with netting bandages to keep the joints mobile. Beware thick bandages.

Prevention is obviously better than cure. Cleanliness is a big plus point. Wash the area scrupulously after every ride and wear clean racing shorts or underpants every time you ride. You may find that ordinary soap doesn't help very much, by the way. Your skin has a certain acidity level which needs to be matched by the soap that you use, otherwise the washing will clear the area of potential infection but lower the resistance for next time. If this sounds like your problem, buy a neutral soap from a chemist. The make I use comes in a green plastic bottle and lasts for ages.

Irritations can be caused by your clothing – especially when you wear several layers during the winter – and by your saddle. Leather saddles very rarely give any trouble; the villains are the plastic ones covered by another layer of plastic or chamois.

What happens is that the covering comes almost imperceptibly loose from the base. You can't detect it when you look at the saddle but your weight and the backward pressure soon create a minor ripple. And that causes the irritation.

If you use an 'artificial' saddle, do try changing it, even temporarily, if you're plagued by a run of saddle boils.

Treatment of boils is slow and gentle – regular washing, of course, and perhaps increased vitamin B in your diet. Brewer's yeast tablets are a good supplement and quite cheap. You can buy them in brown glass bottles of several million at a time from chemists.

Never squeeze a saddle boil. You may extract some of the pus, but you'll also spread it into the surrounding tissue, so that more boils pop up elsewhere. Bring the boil to a head by applying steaming hot flannels for as long as you can bear and applying anti-bacterial ointment.

If despite all this the boil continues to grow, or you're plagued by endless series of the things, see your doctor straightaway.

The remainder of a cyclist's ailments are usually more straightforward, even if they're sometimes no easier to sort out. Backache, for example, is often a sign of weak muscles; you're asking them to hold you in one position for hours on end and in the long run they're just not up to the job and they protest. The answer: strengthen those particular muscles with weight training.

You've only got to look at a collection of cyclists to realise that most of them have relatively well-developed leg and buttock muscles but weak upper bodies. The body needs to work as a cohesive whole, with all the muscle groups working together in balance, so it's hardly surprising your neck or shoulders ache if you haven't done anything to help them.

It's worth looking at your position on the bike as well. If that is too far wrong, you are inviting problems. Are your legs just a fraction bent when the pedal's at the bottom of the stroke? Are your handlebars lower but not ridiculously lower than your saddle (although note that the difference between saddle and handlebar height will be greater for tall riders than short ones)? Is your saddle horizontal, as it should be, and not tilted upwards? Are your handlebars too deep (a common error when some particular superstar, such as Eddy Merckx, sets a fashion that suits him but very few others)? And so it goes on.

The other everyday problems — knee pains, numbness in the hands or feet, for example — are usually fairly easily sorted out. You could check the evenness of your shoeplates — and their straightness — if you have knee pains; you could lower your gears, or alter your saddle height.

Treat the first signs of knee pain with ice packs, warm baths and a rest. You could also make sure you wear training bottoms in all but the very hottest weather, and training bottoms plus long johns for anything colder than chilly.

Numbness usually results from pressure on the nerves for sustained periods, linked to the vibration. You could try padding your bars more, altering their position a bit — the width, for example — or you could try wearing thicker track mitts.

If any of these problems persist, you need to consult a doctor. The trouble is that the doctor rarely needs to see you. Doctors working in the National Health Service are there to cure the sick and, however much you may be inconvenienced, you're not sick. You're actually a very fit and healthy human being for whom the obvious cure is to stop doing whatever is aggravating you — namely cycling — and getting on with a normal life like all the rest of the doctor's patients.

Of course, you may be lucky. There are doctors who are interested in serious athletes, just as there are doctors who collect stamps or go to ballroom dancing lessons. But it'd be silly to pretend they're thick on the ground.

Of course, if you weren't a healthy bike rider you'd be seeing your doctor more often and so you might persuade him to take an interest in your seriousness as an athlete. But unfortunately you're too healthy for that, so you need another ploy. My advice is to see him for anti-tetanus injections, which will intrigue him since few patients volunteer for jabs they don't apparently need.

'Well, golly me,' he'll say, so astonished that he'll drop his stethoscope, 'why in heaven's name do you want those?' And you launch into your 'Well, actually I'm a racing cyclist, you see, and . . .' routine.

Don't overdo it. He doesn't want to sense strident fanfares from on high. He really doesn't care. He's a lot more interested in sticking a needle in your arm, but at least it's a start.

Another word of advice: don't go to the surgery on the busiest night. Find out when it's likely to be quietest. It's a gamble whether an early appointment is better than a late one. He's fresh with an early one, but he's also got a queue of bunions and backs waiting for him. By the end of the evening he's got more time, but he's knackered and his wife's already got the Horlicks on. Who knows?

Failing all this, just a few hospitals have an athletes' clinic, at which you might or might not have to pay. It won't be a fortune, anyway. Phone your nearest large hospital and ask for advice.

A lot of the physiotherapists who work with professional football clubs also run clinics and it's worth phoning the nearest ground. You'll have to pay, of course, but they can't charge outrageous prices or they'd be out of business. Maybe you'd do better at a third or fourth division club. Try it and see.

The one thing that a sports physiotherapist will realise, and which many doctors won't, is that cycling and other sports injuries sometimes need non-standard treatment. A bona fide physiotherapist may not be a cycling expert, but he will certainly be a body expert, and that's all you ask.

19 Step this way...

It was Crystal Palace, I think, and there was a coaches' seminar going on. The fashion of the month was lab tests on the riders we each looked after, the idea being that you could put your guinea-pig on a fixed bike and measure everything there was to be measured. You could see his heart beating on an oscilloscope, you could measure the oxygen he used with a plastic bag, and you could make him ride faster and harder until he was about to drop. And then you told him he was unfit.

What you got at the end of it all was a computer print-out of impressive proportions, and quite unintelligible. Still, these places were around and we were determined to get our blokes there if we could.

So there we were, all wondering how we were going to persuade some boffin to lend us his time, when up got some sage with a sun-tanned bald head and a blazer.

'Of course, gentlemen,' he purred, 'you realise that there are dozens of fitness tests available to you each week, don't you? All you do is put your rider into a race and if he doesn't win, you know he's not fit enough.'

Well, it's true, you know. But wouldn't you just love to get to one of those test labs all the same?

One of the things they can do there is measure just how your heart performs under effort.

Until fairly recently they only knew what it did once you'd stopped, for the simple reason that that was the only time they could get their hands on you. And by that time you'd started to recover anyway.

Then the telemeter came along and they could see for themselves how the heart reacted to exercise, particularly to oxygen debt. The heart's actions were translated into the squiggles that indicate the electrical waves recorded on an electrocardiograph machine.

They found that as your heart beats faster, the rhythm becomes disturbed. The electrical currents have more trouble getting across the heart's fibres. Eventually the heart chambers start opening and closing in the wrong order and the squiggles straighten out for a moment as your heart skips a beat.

Dr Travers and others reckon that the missed beat effect disappears as soon as you ease up. He doubts it'd affect a healthy heart – do it any harm, I mean – but there could be some stress on one with a hidden disease. For that reason, he says, bikies who are going to go beyond steady-state training – in other words, anyone planning to race – should have an electrocardiograph test at a hospital. I'd say that was especially important for older riders – 35 or more, say.

There is no way that exercise can damage a *healthy* heart provided it's not middle-aged and unused to sudden exercise. But disease which may show no symptoms under normal conditions can become painfully clear when provoked. For that reason, it's essential to have a hospital test.

There have been many general tests devised over the years to monitor athletes' fitness. Most of them have a points scale for a standard amount of work. The drawback is that any test is easier for some people than for others; it's easier for someone with long legs to step on and off a bench than for someone with short legs, for instance. And obviously your weight will come into it as well.

What's more, it is possible to become proficient at the test rather than becoming particularly fitter, but there's nothing much we can do about that. Do try the tests if you want to, but remember that the score you achieve won't compare very fairly with what someone else gets. Still, the results could be interesting.

Harvard step test

This was originally a way of measuring the fitness of recruits for the American army. It was devised at Harvard University. The idea is to step on and off a 20-inch-high bench at the rate of one step up and down every two seconds, neither faster nor slower, for a period of five minutes.

It's important that the bench is exactly 20 inches high if you want to check yourself on the basic chart and, whether you do or whether you don't, it's crucial to make sure you go up and down exactly every two seconds. Slower or faster, or any change of pace in between, will affect the score.

Begin by standing in front of the bench (20 inches usually means two standard gym benches, one on top of the other) and step up without pulling on anything with your arms. Stand up straight on top of the bench with your knees unbent, then step down again to finish by standing with straight legs once more in the starting position. Keep your arms straight by your sides all the time.

Step up and down in this manner for five minutes exactly – get a friend to time you and to keep your rhythm.

At the end of the allotted time, take your pulse rate by holding the carotid artery on the side of your neck and recording the number of beats as follows:

1 to $1\frac{1}{2}$ minutes after the exercise ends;
2 to $2\frac{1}{2}$ minutes after the exercise ends;
4 to $4\frac{1}{2}$ minutes after the exercise ends.

Add all the pulse rates together and divide them into 15,000; the result is your physical fitness index, and you can check it against this score list:

Excellent	more than 110
Very good	95–110
Good	88–94
Average	81–87
Fair	75–80
Poor	71–74
Very poor	less than 71

To all intents and purposes, a good bike rider must be in the 'excellent' range. The great runner Emil Zatopek, the first top athlete to use interval training, scored right off the chart – 172 – although on a 17-inch bench.

Tests at Leeds University produced these average figures:

Champion athletes	108.6
Champion swimmers	122.9
University students	79.8

Remember that a test like this is a measure of some vague, general fitness rather than your specific cycling fitness. And it also demands skill so it's also partly a test of your proficiency at performing the Harvard step test, wherein lies its inaccuracy.

Chin–dip–curl test

The step test is a challenge to your heart and lungs, so it measures your cardiovascular ability. The CDC is more of a muscular endurance test, measured in terms of localised movements of the arms and shoulders in relation to body weight, and by trunk curls.

Chins: Adjust a beam so that you can just touch the lower edge. Jump to overhang (knuckles towards you) from the beam. Now, without kicking, jerking or swinging, pull yourself up until your chin is level with the top of the beam. Pulling up to half distance counts half a point (up to a maximum of four points) and each complete pull counts as one.

Dips: Adjust parallel bars to just lower than shoulder height and stand at the end of the bars, grasping one in each hand. Now jump to high support position and count one point. Lower yourself slowly by bending the elbows outwards until your upper and lower arms form a right angle. Then push up into a straight-arm position; this counts as two points. If the straight-arm or right-angle position is not reached, count just one point, up to four points.

Trunk curls: Lie on your back with your palms resting on the tops of your thighs. Pull your chin in and raise your head and shoulders off the floor, slide your hands down your thigh until you can touch your knee caps, then uncurl to lie down again. Make sure you unwind completely.

The time limit in each case is one minute.

	Chins	Dips	Trunk curls
Excellent	13+	18+	48+
Very good	11–13	15–18	38–48
Good	7–10	11–14	28–37
Average	4–6	7–10	19–27
Fair	2–3	4–6	11–18
Poor	1	2–3	6–10
Very poor	0	0–2	0–6

20 And now for success

All that remains for me to say is, believe in yourself. Think in terms of success, never of defeat. Whatever your standard, you haven't yet reached your potential. You can always do better. You could always have done better.

If you don't believe me, look back at the record books. Imagine what a fuss there must have been when the hour fell for the first time in a '25'. Or when Ray Booty broke four hours for 100 miles. And yet now the '25' record is more than ten minutes faster; a four-hour '100' is no longer anything remarkable.

It's not just cycling. Look at the agony on Roger Bannister's face as he beats four minutes for the mile. Now, four minutes is nothing to a good miler; even a 17-year-old schoolboy has beaten it.

You can beat your personal best if you believe that it's nothing more than a fence to be jumped. If you've trained properly, completely, you know that nobody is better prepared than you are. Others may already be further along the path of progression, but that same path is open to you as well. You have the mental approach to accept nothing but success.

Everything a champion does must be in terms of winning. He starts a race not just to finish but to win it, to prove what he already knows. If he doesn't win then he thinks not of failure but of temporary non-success. He thinks positively while others think negatively.

That frame of mind is generated on and off the bike. The old athletics coach Percy Cerutty urged his runners to imagine themselves winning, to live out their imaginings. Their imagination, he said, must be as vivid as a hallucination so that they were mentally accustomed to winning and expected success even before they pulled on their running spikes.

If you've ever had to ask yourself what you need to sacrifice to become a champion, you've lacked the mental approach to get there. A champion sacrifices nothing. He knows he has as much choice as the next man. He has *chosen* bike racing and he has *chosen* to win, to be the best. He is merely exercising that choice.

Every minute spent training is not a minute sacrificed; it's a vital minute chosen for that purpose because it means another step towards success.

Real stars can win any way – from a sprint or alone. Jan Raas was one of those rare all-rounders. (Note Belgian TV's obsession with taking pictures of the riders' feet going round.)

Every man is free to spend his time as he wishes. But people who opt for drinking, smoking and the rest can't understand how an athlete feels, what his higher ideals are, what he yearns for. If they heard that the athlete – you – is dedicated to beating the record of human performance, they might laugh. But the laughter hides the fear of something unknown; the fear of what they themselves could do if they had the motivation. The athlete condemns the ordinary man because he knows he shows him up as a shabby shadow of himself. So the ordinary man must laugh at the athlete because he has to make the athlete seem less than he is. Then the contrast isn't so painful.

There is usually something aloof in the manner of top athletes; not unfriendliness or bigheadedness, just a sense of being more than your everyday human being. With fellow athletes, that aloofness doesn't show.

Let's think again of the champion's attitude to success. For him, there's no such thing as failure. He is like a man crossing a stream by means of stepping stones. The occasions when he gets his feet wet are only indications that he was not successful; he doesn't think of them as failures, only signs that he's still working towards his next target – the next stepping stone. So every temporary non-success is contributing experience that will help him in reaching the next stone. He never doubts that he'll succeed.

The stones are a good analogy. The ultimate target is the far bank of the stream. He knows he'll get there eventually. He's been shown and he's found through training that given a correct technique, he can jump from one stone to the next with reliability. Each stone is a stage towards ultimate success, but also each stone is a success in itself. From the moment our stream-crosser knows he'll reach the far shore, he's across the chasm that divides champions from ordinary men. He has the faith in his ability that will produce exceptional performance to achieve total success.

It's the same in cycling, although sometimes the stones aren't so clear. Maybe they're club schoolboy championship, division schoolboy championship, club and division junior championship, club senior championship, division senior championship, a place in the national championship, selection for national teams, national championship, professional, good professional, top professional and finally world champion. Club schoolboy championship and world championship are the banks of a stream and the gap between them is enormous. Yet the gaps from stone to stone are smaller. It's because the way's not always signposted, and because the opposite bank is sometimes shrouded in mist, that many folk lose their way.

Of course, you may choose a narrower stream. It doesn't matter. Once you've got the outlook of a champion, then you are a champion. Your stream may be individual minutes off your '25' time. It doesn't matter. You create your own stream through your ambition; you take the stepping stones through your training. The world is full of men who don't know where they're going and yet seem surprised when they don't get anywhere.

Sometimes it's hard; sometimes it's just awful. Paul Sherwen grits the gravel in Paris-Roubaix.

There are many barriers along the path to success. Barriers of straw. They look impressive, impregnable. They frighten many people off. But they just need a good hard push.

Perhaps someone 'always' wins your club road race championship, or the club BAR. Admit it and you're beaten from the start. A champion wouldn't even acknowledge his superiority. He's just a stepping stone on your way to success.

From today, never allow yourself to beat yourself. Never give in because someone is ahead of you. That is failure. Press on and finish, knowing that you may have come second, or tenth, or last, but that you've wrenched every last drop from yourself to get that far. That is just temporary non-success.

Quit and you can never do worse. Finish last and you know you've at least beaten the quitters. That's a success. You've reached the first stepping stone while the others are still on the bank. So in finishing, even last, you have succeeded. There is one less stone between you and the far bank.

In the mist that swirls around the stones, it's often not easy to see which stone you're on. Often you can only see how far you've got by looking back, by realising that people you once respected are now your equals. Once you thought you'd never beat them; now you accept them like yourself. No one but yourself can stop you stepping on and past them.

Finally, now you're a champion, remember to act like one. Never lose your temper. If you do, you've lost control of yourself and abandoned all the control and breeding that being a champion has developed. Never forget that you have a responsibility to those with whom you share the roads and the world; don't swear or shout and gesticulate. And always remember those who helped you – the friends and the coach who'll never get the limelight that you'll enjoy, will never get the rewards, will never even experience at first hand the joy you get from winning. Don't forget them.

If you want a code to live by as a cycling champion, take these words that Fausto Coppi, the Italian *campionissimo*, wrote to the Carpano team way back in 1958. They quickly became known as the eight commandments of the champion of champions.

1 Good manners are the first requisite of the rider.
2 Show your education by the control of your tongue and by your bearing. A rider doesn't have to be a dandy, but he should be properly dressed.
3 A rider must honour all the engagements for which he has signed.

4 Courtesy is the sign of a rider conscious of his responsibilities.
5 Politeness is the foundation of all education.
6 The journalist is the representative of public opinion. The rider is responsible in contact with the press for his own standing, and he should help it do its job without ever seeking flattery.
7 Loyalty distinguishes a great rider, in competition and outside it.
8 A rider must control his nerves in all circumstances and must accept good and bad luck with equal serenity.

Ten years ago I said that those words should be printed on the back of every racing licence. I stand by my words.

Index